Claire
The Tutor's Ghost Stories

Rod Galindo

v2.0

TIN
CAN

An imprint of Wordwraith Books

ISBN-13: 978-1-946921-00-0
ISBN-10: 1946921009

Wordwraith Books, LLC
705-B SE Melody Lane #147
Lee's Summit, MO 64063
www.wordwraiths.com
@Wordwraiths

Cover art by The Cover Collection
www.thecovercollection.com

Rod Galindo's website www.rodgalindo.com
Rod Galindo's Twitter @RodAGalindo

This story is dedicated to everyone who fell in love with Max and Claire in their very first short adventure, "The Tutor", just like I did.

It was you, not me, who drew their complete story from the ethereal plane.

Thank you for checking out my novel, I hope you enjoy it!

Allow me to send you the first three chapters from my upcoming novel, **Distress Call.**
Simply hop over to RodWerks.net/SecretSC and tell me where to send it! ☺

For more information on upcoming projects and books, please visit RodGalindo.com

The Stories

1
The Tutor

2
Discovery

3
Awakening

4
The House

5
Departure

6
Return

7
A New Family

8
The Neighbor

9
The Ghost
Hunters, Part I

10
The Ghost
Hunters, Part II

11
The Ghost
Hunters, Part III

12
Unending

1

The Tutor

"Max, look at number seventeen again."

"Why? What's wrong with it?"

Claire fell silent.

He looked again. "Oh. I always do that!" He ground the eraser into the paper.

"Easy, you'll leave a pink smudge!"

Max corrected his mistake and slammed his pencil onto the desk. "Why can't I remember this stuff? Why is it so easy for you?"

"I don't know. I've just always been good at math. When I was your age I won a math bee."

"Really? They had math bees back then?"

"Oh of course! We even had words for our carts and buggies." Claire gave him a sideways look.

"That's not what I meant! I'm sorry, please don't get mad at me."

"Don't worry, Max, I'm only teasing. I could never be mad at you. Okay, next question."

"Can we take a break, please?" Max rubbed his head with both hands. "My brain hurts."

Claire chuckled. "Sure."

"Tell me another ghost story!"

"Oh Max, I think I've told you every one I know a dozen times now. Aren't you tired of hearing them?"

"Claire, I'll never get tired of your stories. But wait a minute!" He turned on the small lamp at his desk, bolted to the bedroom door, switched off the overhead light, and planted himself back in his chair in a flash. "Now I'm ready!"

"Okay. Which one do you want to hear tonight?"

"You pick."

"Alright." Claire cleared her throat and began in her prettiest voice. "Once there was a pretty red-headed girl who lived in an old house on—"

"Oh no, not this one!"

"You said I could pick."

"But this one's so sad!" He looked behind him at the now-darkened room. "And it scares me more than the others."

"Oh, but it's my favorite one, Max. And isn't that the whole point of a ghost story? To scare you?"

Max sighed. "Okaaay."

"Okay." Claire smiled and sat up straight. "Once there was a beautiful red-headed girl who lived in an old house on Hollow Street with her parents and her dog, Rex. On the property just over the creek lived the boy of her sixteen-year-old dreams. She had never known a time without him. They went to school together, they rode horses together, they shared their first kiss together..."

"Ugh, can we skip the mushy parts this time?"

Claire tilted her head. "Someday you might not mind so much."

"Yeah well that 'someday' is not today."

"Fine."

Truth be told, she was right; Max didn't mind the mushy stuff anymore. But of course he couldn't tell her that.

"So one bright summer day, she met him out by the stables. She had bad news. 'We have to move,' she told him. 'In two weeks. My father's job is moving him to Baltimore.' 'As in Massachusetts?' the boy asked without looking up. 'I guess,' the girl replied. "It's Maryland." Max rolled his eyes. "Yes, you're very smart, Max, now hush. She didn't know where Baltimore was, but she knew she didn't want to go. 'I hope we can spend more time together between now and then,' she told the boy, 'I might not ever see you again.' He still didn't look at her. He just brushed his horse with more vigor."

Max took a cracker from the plate his mother had left on his desk. Nibbling helped to calm his nerves during stories like this one.

"'Don't be mad,' she pleaded," Claire continued. "'I don't want our last days together to be full of anger.' 'I'm not mad,' the boy replied, and grabbed her arms really hard and pulled her to him. The girl told him he was hurting her, and he immediately quit squeezing, but she never forgot how violent he could be. 'I'm sorry, I didn't mean to hurt you,' he lied. 'I'm just so mad! I would do anything if it meant you didn't have to leave. Anything.'"

"I hate that guy," Max whispered, narrowing his eyes.

"Then he kissed her," said Claire, closing her eyes.

Max saw her peek before continuing, but he pretended not to notice, instead focusing on the cracker.

"He kissed her so gently it made her toes curl and her hair stand on end. He had the most wonderful kisses in the world. Each one made her forget the hurt."

Max cleared his throat.

Claire sighed. "The girl spent every day with him, and cried every night." Here Claire opened her eyes fully and stared into Max's. "Until her last day finally came."

Max nibbled faster.

She stood from the small bench and sauntered around the desk. "'Today's my last day here,' she told the boy at the fence between their properties. Neither said a word for a long time. The boy finally asked, 'Can I come over tonight and see you? Just us? One last time?' 'Sure!' the girl exclaimed, and was so, so happy she would get to spend one last eve alone with him."

Max shifted in his seat, and ate the rest of his cracker whole. He looked around the room. The corners of his bedroom were almost black. Four human-like turtles stared back at him from the far wall, their faces twisted in anticipation of a fight, ninja-style weapons at the ready. Lightning flashed outside his window, and the wind picked up. Maybe I should have left the light on?

Max turned back to see Claire smiling at him. "What?" A delicate sound of thunder rolled in the distance. He stuffed two crackers in his mouth at once and rubbed his sweaty palms.

Claire bent over the desk and leaned in close, continuing the story in a whisper. "That night, a sound outside startled her. She put down the book she had been reading—Alice's Adventures in Wonderland, her favorite—turned off her bedside lamp, and crept slowly towards the half-open window. The curtains billowed gently in the breeze. The faint scent of the elderberry bush her father planted for supposed medicinal purposes wafted inside. The snap of a twig froze her in her tracks."

Max could not help but gasp, even though he'd heard the story a dozen times.

"Was it her lover?" Claire asked rhetorically. "A burglar? The bogie man?"

"Oh please, we both know it's not the boogie man," Max said, his nerves calming a bit. He took a drink to get rid of the cotton-mouth that too many crackers in a row does to a person.

"Who's telling this story?"

Max swallowed the last of the water and set the empty glass on the desk without a sound.

"I'll never get over the funny way children say 'boh-gie' these days," said Claire. "Anyway, you're right, it was indeed the boy!"

Max rolled his eyes.

"She was so happy to see him! He ever-so-quietly climbed in through the window and hugged her warmly." Claire drew her arms to her chest and spun once, coming to a stop in middle of the large rug in the center of the room. "'I have to tell you something,' her lover said. And then his head snapped toward the bedroom door. The girl, afraid, did the same." Claire also jerked her head in the direction of Max's bedroom door, exactly as her characters did in her story. "'Did you hear something?' she asked the boy. 'My father may have awoken—' He pulled her closer, interrupting her train of thought. 'Sweetheart,' the boy said, 'I have found a way to keep you here. I got the idea from William. You don't have to leave, we can be together. Forever.' 'Really?' the girl replied. 'How? Who's William?' Then the boy set his palm firmly in the center of her back, and stared into her wide, green eyes. 'A poet. And a friend.' He put his soft, wet lips to her ear. 'Trust me,' he whispered. 'I trust you,' she replied, barely even hearing her own voice. Then his lips met hers once again. This one, this kiss... oh, it was a terribly passionate kiss. The best one yet. The best one ever. Light. Feathery. Tender. His touch was absolutely—"

"Mushyyy!" Max held the last syllable long enough to remind her.

Claire took a deep breath. "You can really ruin a beautiful moment, you know that, Max?" She gave him a look that would kill most boys where they stood.

Max slumped in his chair. Please calm down. Please calm down.

She closed her eyes.

Please, please, please...

"She lost herself in that kiss," Claire continued, eyes still closed. "She lost everything in that one, glorious moment. And then something pierced her heart. It was cold. Like ice." Claire opened her eyes wide. "The girl's eyes shot open, and she screeeeeamed."

Max was ready. He smashed his sweaty palms to his ears as hard as he could, but it barely helped. Claire let out her signature high-pitched banshee howl, the one that always turned Max's toes into fists and raised the goosebumps all over his body. But this one was different. Max had never heard her let loose like this before. The scream went on and on, and made the empty glass on his desk sing all by itself. Claire was really putting on a show for him tonight! Her mouth finally closed, and the soul-stealing scream died away. Max's hands shook when he released the death-grip he had on his own head.

Claire went on. "'I love you,' the boy told the girl. She went limp. He lowered her to the floor. She lay there, staring at the open window. A tangy, coppery scent replaced the sweet smell of elderberries. The room spun as her vision began to fade. A moment later, her One True Love collapsed upon her, his face next to hers. A bloody kitchen knife clanged on the wooden floor and came to rest just out of reach. The girl couldn't move. 'I will love you forever,' he whispered. And then, everything went black."

Max heard footsteps outside his bedroom door. Someone was roaring his way. His heart pounded in his throat. Muffled voices reached his ears. What are they saying?

He made fists to stop his quivering fingers. He looked at Claire and waited.

She seemed nonplussed, ignoring the footsteps and the voices. She wasn't finished.

This wasn't the end of the story.

"Then," Claire said, "to her great surprise, the girl woke up! She wasn't alive, but she wasn't entirely dead, either. She was alone. Alone in that big, old, creaky house." She turned her head and stared out the window. "She never saw the boy again. Nor her parents. She saw Rex though, and he saw her. And they played together often, until the little dog finally died. Then they played less often. And eventually, the girl was completely alone."

Max's eyes usually teared up at this point, but they didn't tonight. His eyes flashed between Claire and the bedroom door. The muffled voices had stopped.

"To this day, the girl still roams the halls of that old house on Hollow Street, searching for her lost love. For the boy who made sure she never left that house. The boy who murdered her..."

The footsteps outside resumed their stomping. Coming closer. Claire had turned, her entire body now fixated on Max's bedroom door.

He swallowed hard, and prepared himself for anything that might come through—

The door flung open wide. Max jumped out of his skin and nearly fell out of the chair. He stared, mouth agape, at the pale figure looming before him in the doorway.

"Max, is everything alright in here? Max! Are you okay?"

He somehow found the strength to breathe again. His shoulders slumped. "Yes, Mom. I'm fine."

Max's mother looked around the room. "Why is it so dark in here? Are you finished with your homework? Did you hear that just now?"

"Hear what?"

"Come on, you can't tell me you didn't hear that scream!"

Max and Claire both shook their heads at the same time.

"Don't play games, now."

"I'm not! It was probably my dumb sister."

"Sophie said it wasn't her, I asked." His mother crossed her arms. "That girl and her room, I swear..."

"Maybe it was the storm?" Max suggested.

Mom cocked her head. "Not even tornadoes sound like that."

Max looked at Claire. Claire looked at Max. They turned to look at the woman in the doorway.

"Oh, nevermind!" Mom finally said. "Your dad's probably watching some silly horror movie downstairs again!" She shook her head. "That ridiculous stereo system of his! Don't worry, I'll make sure he turns it down. He knows you're doing your homework, I don't know why he has to have it so loud! Are you about finished?"

Max turned and glanced at his book. "Yeah, I only have a couple more questions."

"Good, it's after eight thirty. I want you in bed on time tonight, mister. Do you hear me?"

"Yes, Mommm." Another brief flash of lighting filled the room.

Max's mother turned to leave, then paused. "So weird, though. It sounded like the scream came from just down the hall, not downstairs. You honestly didn't hear it?"

"I didn't hear anything," Max said. He looked at Claire, who shrugged her shoulders.

The woman rolled her eyes. "Whatever, okay." Gentle thunder answered the lightning bolt that lit the room few seconds ago. "Oh, Max! I got your Spiderman jammies washed. They're in your dresser there."

Claire giggled.

"Mom!" Max jumped up and grabbed the doorknob.

"Alright, alright, I'm leaving."

He slammed the door shut.

"You make sure to brush your teeth!" his mother called from the hall. "And turn on a light! I don't know how you can possibly see in the dark!"

"Okay!" Max rested his head on the closed door.

"She can't help it," Claire said. "She loves you, that's all."

"Yeah, yeah." Max looked up. His head and shoulders cast a dark shadow on the white door in the lamplight. "You want to play shadow puppets?"

"Okay." Claire said, and appeared beside him.

Max backed away from the door and dropped to his knees to give them more "canvas space" on the door and wall. He intertwined his thumbs the way his father did. An eagle appeared on the wall next to the door.

"So majestic!" his tutor announced.

He made a dog. "Arf, arf!"

Claire smiled and pretended to pet it. "Good puppy!"

Max put his palms together and curled up one index finger. He clapped his hands in rapid succession. "I'm-a-gonna eat you up!" he growled.

"Oh no!" Claire exclaimed. "Don't let that nasty old alligator eat me!" Her red pony tail bobbed from side to side and she raised her hands to protect her beautiful face. "Help me, Max!"

"I'll save you, fair maiden!" He made a dramatic gesture and killed the foul beast.

"Yay! You saved me! The kingdom is safe once again!"

Max smiled at Claire. She was at her loveliest when she smiled, too. And she usually did. But at times she could be terrifying.

"You have such a great imagination, Max," she said. "You can even make something as simple as shadow puppets entertaining!"

Max's smile turned tight-lipped. He looked down at the large rug in the center of the room. Directly underneath was the dark brown spot on the hardwood floor that no one could remove. His gaze then wandered to the dark red stain on Claire's flowery nightgown. He looked up, into those green eyes he was so very fond of. "I only wish you could cast a shadow, too."

2

Discovery

"Claire?" Mrs. Harvey stood quietly, her ear to her daughter's bedroom door. She heard nothing but the sound of her husband's footsteps behind her. "Claire is up, isn't she?"

"Haven't seen her this morning," Mr. Harvey replied on his way down the staircase, carrying the last of the moving crates to the foyer. "But it's still pretty early, you know. She was up late reading; her lamplight shone under the door when I retired for the night."

Mrs. Harvey pursed her lips. "That girl and her darned reading," she muttered. "It had better have been the Bible!" She put a hand on the door frame and listened for movement beyond the door. Do I dare enter uninvited? And break one of my own rules of etiquette?

If she couldn't be a good example, how could she expect her daughter to follow high society's rules? "Claire, dear, are you awake? We need to hurry this morning! The movers will be here at seven to load the last of the furniture and we need to be on the road by noon. I don't want to have to rush to the train station! You know how bumpy it gets when the horses pass a trot." She snapped her fingers and called over her shoulder, "That reminds me, Gerald, did you oil the carriage springs?"

His voice was barely audible from the first floor.

"I'll get to it before we depart, my darling."

"Oh! You've been saying that for two weeks now!"

"Crates didn't pack themselves, my sweet cherry blossom."

"I'll show you sweet," Mrs. Harvey said under her breath. "Claire?"

Still no response.

Mrs. Harvey took a deep breath. "Oh this girl will be the death of me." And, making an exception in this one case, she opened the door.

* * *

Mr. Harvey didn't hesitate when he heard the scream. He dropped the crate he was about to stack and bolted back up the staircase. At the top, he saw his wife at the end of the hall, standing in Claire's bedroom doorway. Before he could reach her, she screamed again. When he looked into the room, his breath caught in his throat. He couldn't move.

The sight. The odor.

Yesterday, Claire's room smelled like elderberries and perfume. Now it was filled with the putrid stench of death. His stomach churned. How? Why? When?

Next to him, his wife shook, her screams now staccato, her breath coming in quick gasps. He grabbed her with both hands before she fell on her face. He coughed and focused on keeping his breakfast down, lest he lose it all over her prettiest traveling clothes. They both dropped hard to the floor, her in his arms, he on one knee. She reached out to her daughter with a hooked hand, her burgundy-hued gloves eerily matching the pool of dark blood under their daughter.

Mr. Harvey held his wife close, trying to pull her into his open suit jacket to shield her from the hideous sight.

"Clairrrre!" Mrs. Harvey heaved and wailed into his chest.

He stared at the body of his once-beautiful little girl. She lay on her back on the hardwood floor in the middle of the room, facing him. Her mouth appeared frozen in a half-scream, her unseeing eyes wide open, her brow slightly knitted as if in disbelief. A dark red stripe went from the corner of her mouth to her ear. Her long auburn hair, splayed out in every direction, was crusted with blood

On top of her lay that blasted neighbor boy, Stephen, the odd one that Mr. Harvey and his wife both knew was trouble from the start. The little monster lay on his stomach, all but crushing little Claire, his eyes also open and staring at the back of her head as if he was within the throes of a dream. As if he was in love. As if he had just given her the greatest gift anyone could give.

Immortality.

You son of a ratbag! Only the Good Lord above can grant such a gift! You! Why, you gave her nothing, but took everything! "You rotten little beast!" he yelled, not caring the boy couldn't hear him. "I hope you burn in the fires of Hell!"

Mrs. Harvey wailed again, and Mr. Harvey shut his mouth, tears now streaming down his cheeks. He was prepared to rock his wife for as long as she needed, partially because he couldn't find the strength to stand anyway.

What is that? Mr. Harvey squinted at an object a short distance away. Is that what I think it is? A bloodied kitchen knife lay in the direction of the monster's outstretched hand. Is that what you used, you worthless, misbegotten ruffler, to take our daughter from us?

Claire's eyes. Her beautiful green eyes. He had to close them.

He had to get that monster off of her.

He had to ride into town and alert the sheriff, then the coroner.

Then he had to unpack his guns. Mr. Chauncey Harvey the Third had unfinished business with the boy's ratbag of a father.

3

Awakening

Claire awoke with a start, hyperventilating. She couldn't stop. Her mind screamed.

What happened?

Where am I?

What time is it?

Her head snapped from side to side, her eyes wild. My room! I'm in my room. Her shoulders slumped, and she caught her breath. Well of course I'm in my room, where else would I be? Her brow knitted. Wait. Is this my room? Where's my bed? Nothing but the walls looked familiar.

A noise came from outside. What was that? Her head jerked toward the window. The light flooding in made her squint, and she shielded her eyes from the glare. Where are the curtains? She identified the sound then. Merely a buggy clamoring down Old Hollow Road, the long dirt road that began somewhere in the rolling hills to the west, and led all the way to King City in the east. It looked to be nearly mid-day. Had she slept on the floor all night? Wait, mid-day!? Claire jumped to her feet. Mother must be furious! Claire remembered her mother telling her over and over how she'd wanted to be on the road immediately after breakfast, so the driver could give them a pleasant and semi-leisurely ride to the train depot.

Looking down she noticed her pale, bare feet contrasted starkly against the dark floorboards. She gasped, and grabbed her nightgown with both hands. My clothes! I must change! She turned toward her towering wardrobe. But it wasn't there. Where in all the world is my traveling couture? The wardrobe that had stood in the corner and housed all her dresses was gone. As was her dresser and vanity. And her bed and nightstand! Along with all her books! But they were just here! How could they—? "The movers!" she said aloud. They must have come while I was asleep and—

"Hold your horses, Claire," she told herself. How could the men have moved everything without waking her up? And how could her mother have let them move all that heavy furniture around her daughter, who was sleeping on the floor? It wouldn't have happened. Never in a hundred years.

Mother. Mother will know where everything is. She arranged all the particulars with the movers, after all. "Mother?" she called.

No answer.

Claire launched herself into the hallway. Since the door to the guest room directly across from her own room was open, she glanced inside. It was empty, but then it had been emptied weeks ago. Halfway down the hall, across from the top of the grand stair, she came to the door to her parents' room, at the very center of the second floor. She opened it and peered inside.

"Father?" It was as empty as her own, the curtains gone from all the windows as well as the French doors leading out to the balcony. "What in the Good Lord's name is going on?" she asked no one. They wouldn't have left without me!

It was the only thought that went through Claire's mind as she ran to the other end of the hall. To her left was the sitting room, normally her second favorite place to read other than under her favorite tree in the meadow behind the house. But there were no longer any big, comfy chairs in which to sit and lose herself in a story. To her right was her father's study, with its inviting, circular floor plan, part of the home's only "tower." Not even a discarded scrap of paper greeted her.

No...

She turned, darted down the hall, flew down the grand staircase, zipped through the foyer, and arrived on the front porch more quickly than she ever had in her life. Old Hollow Road lay just beyond a small set of cement stairs at the end of a short, brick walkway. There was no carriage waiting on the road. She turned and barreled around the house to the barn. If the horses were gone...

But they can't be. Mother simply went ahead in the carriage, that's all. Up ahead, she saw the barn door wide open. Ha! Father is out there right now, readying the smaller buggy to take him and I to the train station! I should have known! I hope he has some clothes for me! That will be embarrassing if—

Claire stopped in her tracks when she reached the open door. The barn was empty. Both the carriage and the buggy were gone, as were all the horses. She shook her head. It can't be. It just can't. Why would they leave me? Why? She turned and looked to the east, toward town, toward where she knew her parents would catch the train to their new life. "Why did you leave me?" she screamed. "Why!?" Her knees hit the ground, and she burst into tears. She bent over and pushed her face into the ground, not caring if she dirtied herself up, like Mother had always told her to be careful not to do. She had nowhere to go now anyway, no reason to look presentable. She lost track of how much time passed as she let it all out until the tears would no longer come.

The sun still hung high in the sky when she trudged back to the front porch. She took a breath of the fresh, Autumn air. It and the bright sunlight cheered her spirits, but only slightly. A thought struck her. She blinked the last of the tears from her eyes, straightened up, and looked around the yard.

"Rex?" she called. She cupped a hand to her brow to block the sun, and peered down the dirt road to the west. "Here, boy!" She looked south, toward Old Man Moody's cornfield. "Rex!" she called again. She didn't expect for him to come; surely her parents had taken him with them when they left.

Claire turned and moped back inside. As she stood in the empty foyer, she imagined she was a sight to behold. She was almost happy the foyer's mirror was gone; her hair was probably a rat's nest, and her eyes had surely never been so red and puffy, at least not since grandpa had died.

She wandered into the kitchen with its empty cupboards. Not a single spoon was forgotten in the partially-open kitchen drawers. She moped through the formal dining room. Only the glass chandelier and the flowery wallpaper remained, the pattern Claire always thought so ugly. It only made her mood worsen. She dragged her bare feet across the foyer to the living room, and behind that into the parlor that, all her life, had sported the large pool table and smoking chairs. All were gone now. Perhaps they're hiding? Maybe to scare me, for fun! That's it, they're just having a bit of fun with me on our last day! But where would they be hiding?

The cellar!

Claire sped back to the kitchen, a smile growing on her face. She blew through the door to the basement, tucked neatly between the kitchen and the dining room, and padded fast down the creaky, narrow, wooden stair. Her bare feet hit the dirt-floor and her smile faded. She was met only by a musty smell. The meager sunlight that filtered in from the small easement windows near the ceiling told her everything she needed to know. The hot water boiler, usually chugging away, was as silent as the brick and mortar walls.

"They really did leave me."

Even in relatively new homes such as this one, cellars always seemed damp. Claire looked down at her feet and crinkled her toes in the cold dirt.

Probably because she had nothing better to do at the moment, she wondered why the builders never bricked up the floor.

A whistle blared in the distance and her heart skipped a beat. The train! Perhaps it's not too late! Perhaps I can catch them! Claire tore back up the stairs and was out the front door in a flash. She barely gave a thought to the front yard, now devoid of ornaments. She leapt over the hedge and onto the dirt road and made her way east, toward the station. Toward her father, one of only four living beings on Earth she truly cared about. There was Father, her horse, the family beagle, and the neighbor boy, Stephen, who she would surely marry someday.

She was nearly even with the barn before she felt her legs brushing against her nightgown, and she slowed. Oh, my word! I'm out in the road, in public, in my nightgown! Should she stop? Go back? Go back to what? There wasn't even a set of silverware left in that house, let alone garments of any kind. No. Go on. Catch your family!

She ran.

She ran as fast as her spindly pale legs and bare feet would carry her, staying in the grass to avoid the sharp rocks in the dirt road. The cornfield across the road to her right was a blur. Old man Moody's house was coming up, also off to her right. She hoped and prayed neither he nor his wife would look outside and see her in her—

A pressure fell upon her chest without warning, and shortened her breath. It slowed her a little, but not too much. Then it was gone. Well, that was weird. It then occurred to her she had missed breakfast, so maybe that was it? But she wasn't hungry. She thought that weird, too. It was not only past breakfast, it was past lunchtime! I should be starving!

The feeling struck her again. "Ohhh!" Claire clutched her chest and slowed to a walk. She let out a huff as a stronger bout of pressure gripped her. It was a weight upon her, trying to collapse her lungs. Her brows came together in confusion. She had barely reached the end of Moody's cornfield, the start of his yard, and already she was out of breath?

Her pace slowed further, but not by choice. It was as if she was running through mud, but the ground wasn't wet. She wanted to move her feet faster, but simply couldn't. She took a few more steps before a dull ache shot through her, going from the base of her skull to the pit of her stomach. "What—?" she gasped. "What is going on?" Claire's hand first went to the back of her neck. It wasn't a headache per se, but it was definitely something. It hurt. But her chest hurt more. Then her back. She didn't know what to do with her hands. She couldn't study the part of her that hurt because the pain was everywhere.

Old man Moody stood in the yard beside the house, chopping wood. Had he seen her? Probably not; the corn had blocked Claire's view of him up to this point. Surely he would stop and stare with a slack jaw if he caught sight of a nightgowned teenager out for an absolutely inappropriate stroll down the road in the middle of the day! She decided that if he saw her, she would wave, just to be neighborly. She didn't want to, especially if this would be the last time she ever saw him before catching the train to Baltimore. Wait. This is the last time I will see him, before leaving for good! So what did it matter if he saw her or not? She would wave unabashedly and defiantly of conservative tradition. And hold her head high when she did so. Or at least she would, if pain wasn't wracking her body. Her pace now hit a snail's crawl. It was as if she were moving through molasses. The short distraction of Farmer Moody had been enough for her not to notice the aching had now spread to her fingers and toes. She remembered her grandma suffering from arthritis. Is this what that was like? But how and why would she be experiencing such a thing? At sixteen?

Anxiety filled her gut, and she ground to a halt. Her breathing quickened. Her heart pounded in her ears. Her skin felt battered and bruised. Tendons were suddenly sprained out of nowhere. Her internal organs seemed as though they would burst. More-less every ailment she could image all rolled into one! "What in the world?"

She dared not take another step forward. She looked over at Old Man Moody, busily chopping his wood. He seemed not to notice her. Maybe he can help? She started toward him, but her feet wouldn't move. She tried to call out, but her voice caught in her throat. Claire closed her eyes and waited for the feeling to pass, but it didn't.

She forced every muscle in her legs into motion, and managed to take a step backward. Then another. And a few more. The pain. Was it letting up? She couldn't be sure, but it was easier to move now. She clamored backward faster, her eyes still closed. She didn't think about falling backward until she was in mid-air.

She landed hard in the grass, but thankfully missed catching the back of her head on the barbed wire fence that ran the length of the road. The impact pushed a yelp out of her. It didn't hurt as much as she had expected. In fact, it didn't really hurt at all. The odd sensation flowing through her body hurt a lot more. Maybe it was overpowering the pain of landing on her tailbone?

Old Man Moody continued to slam his axe through logs, splitting them into pieces small enough to fit into his fireplace. He either ignored or didn't notice what was going on across the street, not a stone's throw away.

Claire squinted and raised a hand to block the noon-time sun. It was then she noticed a thin man standing in the window of an upper bedroom of Moody's house. It didn't look like the oldest son, Abraham Moody, but Claire determined it must be.

"Mr. Moody?" she called through a still slightly constricted throat. He didn't reply. She looked back to the man in the window. Was it even a man? It more resembled a mannequin than a real person. But it was unlike any Claire had seen at the Sears store in town. Most of those had been lady mannequins, wearing the utmost in modern fashion. This one wore overalls and a dingy white t-shirt underneath, in stark contrast to the "gentleman" dummies, who wore business suits and leisure wear. But why would Old Man Moody have a mannequin at all, let alone one dressed in such a way? "Mr. Moody!" she called again, more forcefully this time. She made the painful climb to her feet, not caring about scruples anymore.

He continued to ignore her.

"Mr. Moody, is that Abraham? Up in the window?" It pained her to speak, but she needed help. Because of this incredibly awkward situation, she had no idea how to proceed in a socially-acceptable manner, so she continued with small talk. " I didn't know he had returned from Africa. When did he get back?"

Moody chopped and chopped. He was being very rude this morning! Maybe he didn't know how to act in such an awkward situation, either? Perhaps he had already seen her, saw what she was wearing, and didn't want to embarrass her? I can respect that. I guess.

The mannequin was gone when her eyes fell upon the window again, and her breath caught. So it was a real man! It had to be Abraham. She looked back at Old Man Moody. "Mr. Moody, please, I need help! My parents have—"

He slammed the axe hard into the stump one last time, and began collecting cords of wood. Her shoulders slumped. "Fine, ignore me!" she hollered. "Who cares if I'm in pain!"

Her yelling ceased when she saw Abraham again. This time in another window, one floor up and on the other end of the house. He only stared at her, as he did before. She peered hard at him this time. He looked ill. Pale. His jaw opened, then shut. Then opened again. But it didn't look as though he was trying to talk. It was more like a yawn, but without any of the stretching or eye squishing that people did when they yawned. And his eyes, they looked...

A chill went up her spine. "Mr. Moody!" she hissed. "Why is your son acting so strangely?"

Moody continued collecting wood in his arms.

"Hey! Old Man Moody!" That was sure to get his attention; he hated being called this. Claire had learned that at age six, and had never forgotten the tongue-lashing that had ensued.

Moody, his arms now full, started toward the side door to the house.

"Why are you so ill-tempered?" she shouted, clutching her side in an attempt to subdue the pain.

Moody pulled the screened-door open with a free finger and struggled to get inside without dropping anything.

Claire looked back up to the windows. The thin man was gone again. "Oh forget it!" Claire turned and started back toward her home, but threw her glance over her shoulder one last time to yell at her neighbor. "Mean Old Man Moody—" Her throat clenched up and she stumbled to a stop. The thin man. He was now on the porch. But she had never heard the front door creak open. The man simply stood there, silent and unmoving, like he had in the windows. In the daylight, Claire could see him better. His skin was ashen, his overalls torn and shabby. His hair disheveled. And those eyes. She had been right; they were as white as a cloudy sky. And there were no pupils, not that she could see, anyway. She tried to keep her face from twisting at the sight of him. "Abraham?" She leaned forward. "Is that you?"

His jaw worked again, and his mouth fell open a little too far. His entire maw was yellowish-brown. Teeth, tongue, everything. His head lurched, and a screeching reached Claire's ears, a sound she had never heard in all her sixteen years.

She smashed her palms against either side of her head, but it didn't help to drown out the high-pitched racket. And then the thin man's jaw snapped shut, and the unnatural noise ceased.

That's not Abraham.

Claire couldn't move. The door to the side of the house banged shut, and her glance shot to its location. Mr. Moody was back outside, looking around, then up into the sky. He had heard it! Well of course he did, who wouldn't hear such a thing?

But then Moody did something odd. He shrugged, and went back to collecting the last of the firewood.

Claire's brow furrowed. When she looked back in the thin man's direction, he was now by the mailbox, right across the road.

This nearly made her stumble backward. How did you get there so fast? "Mr..." Her mouth opened, but only short breaths came out. "Moody...? Abraham Moody?"

The man leaned toward Claire. He looked angry. His mouth flew open, and yet another screech burst forth.

Claire no longer cared if Old Man Moody heard that one or not. She turned and ran. She reached the front porch at full speed. She didn't remember opening the front door, but she was inside, safe from the thin man's blind gaze.

Even though the house was completely empty and looked nothing like it did only yesterday, with all the large, oak furniture and all the moving crates scattered about, it was still her home. But the drastic difference between the warm environment it had been during her childhood and the way it looked now broke her heart. But it was a safe place.

Or was it?

She whirled around and grabbed the deadbolt. It seemed stuck at first, but she gritted her teeth, and snapped the handle into place with a violence that surprised her. Then she rested her forehead on the door and took deep, purposeful breaths to calm herself. The crippling pain that had gripped her earlier was completely gone. Was it anxiety? Why had her anxiety been so overpowering she couldn't even make it to the train station? It wasn't like her. She'd walked to the general store a thousand times on her own and never experienced any kind of fear. Okay, maybe not a thousand times, but a lot! And forget the anxiety, what was that pain and nausea all about? Now it was all gone, like it had never happened. She padded to the top of the stairs and turned toward her bedroom. Just before her room, on the right, was the home's only bathroom. When a normally ordinary thought crossed her mind, she stopped at the doorway. *Have I gone to the bathroom yet this morning?* It wasn't such an ordinary thought today. She always had to use the toilet first thing in the morning. Everyone did. *Didn't they?* But she didn't remember having to today. And she didn't have to now. *So odd.* She stepped into the oversized room and stood before the mirror. Her hair was indeed a mess, and her skin looked like it was recovering from a sunburn. "Woah." *I must have got more sun than I remembered on my ride yesterday!* She touched her nose and forehead, which were peeling the most. Her hand instinctively went to the drawer where the skin cream was normally kept, but the drawer wouldn't budge. Her lips pursed and she pulled until she thought the knob would come off in her hand, but it didn't. "Oh!" she said under her breath. "It's stupid, Claire, it wouldn't matter anyway!" Surely the drawer was as empty as the cupboards downstairs. She stood there a moment staring at herself, until a memory zipped through her brain. In the mirror, her eyes grew to the size of saucers.

Claire bolted out the door and around the corner into her bedroom, diving for a small panel in the wall between her room and the bathroom. The tiny, metal latch was in place, as expected, but today she had a hard time lifting the small bolt and chain. It felt as if it weighed a ton. She gritted her teeth again. She had to get it open, she just had to! She stood and yanked on the chain, and it eventually came free. She let out a breath, and then grabbed for the edge of the small door to open it. But the door was sealed up as tight as the bathroom drawer had been a moment ago.

Her brows came together. She tried again. "Oh come on!" she shouted. "Did someone paint it shut? Who would paint this door shut? It's the only way to get to the valve that turns the water on and off!" As she struggled with the door, she couldn't help but imitate her father. "Whoever designed it like this was an idiot! Why not simply turn the valve around so you could reach it from the other direction, and put the access panel inside the bathroom! Oh, but that would make too much sense!" She giggled at her ability to mimic him so well.

It was rare to hear him talk in such a way. He was only outspoken when something truly bothered him. And when her mother wasn't around; when she was, he was as quiet as a church mouse. Claire suspected he was probably just tired of losing every argument, even when he was right.

She shook off the memory of her father and worked her fingers into the crack between the wooden panel and the wallpaper. "Finally!" Claire pulled, hard, but the door still wouldn't budge. She visually examined the hinges, not daring to let go of the progress she had made. They didn't look rusted or anything. She put her weight into it, leaning backwards as far as she dared. If the little bolt had weighed a ton, the door weighed a thousand pounds. Okay, maybe not a thousand. But probably darn close! "Hmm." She cocked her head to one side. "I don't know why you won't open, but I'm going to fix your little red wagon!" She sat down and braced her feet against the wall. She then dug all her fingers deeper around the hinged panel and leaned back, almost laying on the hardwood floor, and pulled with all her might. A growl arose from deep inside her. Soon it manifested into a full-fledged scream.

Claire nearly fell backwards when the door flew open. She lay there panting for a moment, and let loose a cheer for herself. "Ha!" she hollered. "Take that, you stupid door!" She stuck out her tongue at it like a girl half her age. She sat up and reached inside the opening. In only a second, her hand fell upon the treasure she sought: her jewelry box. She sighed, and her whole body went limp.

Still there.

Claire looked up at the ceiling. "Thank you." The decorative box was light and came out easily. She caressed the pretty painted flowers wrapped around the surface of the small case. Sitting cross-legged on the floor, she lifted the lid, and peered upon all her most precious memories and belongings. The photograph of her and her favorite porcelain doll. Mother must have taken Abby with her when she left for Baltimore. The photo of her and Father when she was fourteen, taken right before the Daddy-Daughter dance at her school. Hopefully someday someone will invent color photography! That dress was so pretty! Her gaze fell upon her wind-up ballerina, from when she was but a wee little thing. Silly, she knew, but she cherished it because it came from Grandma, who'd had it when she herself was a little girl. The paint was coming off the chiseled wood, but that simply gave it character.

She studied the artwork on a miniature matchbox her father had picked up during a long business trip to California. He collected several of these, and displayed them in the parlor. Claire remembered he said he had purchased this particular box in a small mining town called "Las Vegas Rancho" a few years before she was born, in the 1870s. It wasn't in California, but Nevada, where his train had passed through on his way home. An artist had painted a pretty Mexican girl on the top cover, and Claire thought the colors were just beautiful. Her mother had not, apparently. When Claire was about eight years old, her mother had finally tired of looking at "the vulgar thing" and had thrown the matchbox in the trash. Claire rescued it after everyone had left the room, and added it to her collection; she figured no one would notice it missing.

She dug through a few other sentimental trinkets and came across something else that gave her pause. The heart-shaped charm Stephen had given her, with both their photographs on either side. His was one he had stolen from his mother and cut out to fit into the charm. She had sneaked a photo of herself as well. Neither were smiling in their photographs—that would be inappropriate of course—but seeing the images together made her smile.

Wait. Stephen! He'll be able to help! Or at least his parents will!

Claire packed everything away, closed the lid, stuffed the jewelry box back in its hiding place, and tried to shut the door. Of course it wouldn't move. She gave it a kick, but it was no use. "Oh forget it!" she grunted, and ran out of her room and down the hall. She barreled down the stair and turned right upon reaching the foyer that extended nearly to the back of the house. She moved quickly through the always cold "mud room", through the screened-in back porch, and burst onto the sculpted back lawn.

Stephen's house was only a half-mile away, on the next property over, just beyond the meadow. She could partially see his house from her second-story bedroom, but not entirely due to the trees that surrounded it. She reached the edge of her back lawn and plowed through the expanse of native grass of the meadow. It only slowed her a little since it was barely even above her knees. Mr. Branton is smart! I don't care what Father says about him being eccentric, he will surely help me get a wire to Baltimore! Let my parents know I'm safe! Maybe Father can use the telegraph to send money? What is it called again? Wiring money, or something like that? Mr. Branton could buy a train ticket! And Mrs. Branton could help me pick out some new clothes! Oh, why didn't I think of this an hour ago?

A familiar noise came from her left. She slowed down. The noise came again. A low growl. That almost sounds like Rex! But it can't be! Mother would never have left little Rex! Father might have, however... He always thought a beagle was a waste of time. A worthless pet. "What this family needs is a good hunting dog!" he would say, about once a year. Followed quickly by her mother quipping, "As if you have ever hunted in your life!" And then the arguing would start, and Father would say something about regretting ever opening his mouth, and Claire would bury herself in a book, any book, to escape. She tried to push those memories away as the growl came again. "Hey, little fella!" she called, and took a step toward what she was sure was a dog.

The growling intensified.

Claire stood up straight. "Boy, I sure hope you're a dog!" Claire moved her head around as she continued to approach, trying to catch a glimpse of the angry if not frightened animal. She peered into the grass. "It's alright. I'm nice."

As soon as their eyes met, the little beagle froze, and its eyes locked upon hers.

"Rex! It is you!"

The animal's growling turned into whimpering, and the tiny bell hanging from his collar dinged as he cowered and backed away.

"Oh you poor thing!" Claire rushed to him, cupped the dog in her arms, and brought him to her bosom.

Rex yelped and cried continuously.

"Rex! Are you okay? Are you hurt?"

He tried desperately to wiggle free of her grasp.

"Shh, shh, shh, it's okay, it's okay," Claire said, tightening her grip. "Did you get into another fight with a 'coon? Or were you caught in a trap, maybe? Where does it hurt, boy?"

His head turned away from her as he continued to cry, but his eyes kept looking back into hers, again and again.

"Oh, Rex, you can trust me! It's me, after all! Your best friend!"

The dog's cries dropped back to a whimper.

"I don't see any blood," Claire said. She examined each of his paws in turn.

The little dog pulled each one away as she did so.

"Rex! What's gotten into you? You've never acted like this before!"

He yelped again, as if scared when she raised her voice.

"Oh, Rex, it's okay! It's okay, I'm sorry! Shhhhh."

Rex whined and continued to shake, but didn't try to escape her arms again.

Claire looked him all over with brows squished together at the puzzle before her. "Well, Cuddle Bear, I can't see where you're hurt. Not on the outside, anyway." She hugged him, and Rex quieted down. "Did that mean ol' Vincent scare you again? I swear, Farmer Johansen should just put that mangy old mutt down!"

Rex whimpered again.

"Oh, are you thinking I'm mad at you or something? No, no, I could never be mad at you, you sweet little thing. I shouldn't have mentioned that mean old dog's name, should I? No, I shouldn't have!" She hugged the little dog again. "Oh, Rex, you're really shaking bad! What happened that made you so scared?"

Rex glanced up at her and his ears went up every time she asked him a question, but he looked away again and again, seemingly not able to hold her gaze.

"Well, I don't know why you're acting so weird, but I have to get to Stephen's house so his father can send a wire to Father!" She stood up, cradling the dog. "Come on, you can come with me. I'm sure Mrs. Branton will have a nice chunk of meat you can have, and a big bowl of water! Who knows when the last time you ate was!"

Rex didn't protest.

She walked on through the grass, the dog seeming to calm down somewhat. "You'll be okay soon, Rex, you'll see. You're just traumatized like I am because our parents left us! Now, I'll be honest with you. I can see why my father might have left you, but I can't see how mother could have left either of us! She's simply not—

Claire halted in her tracks. The anxiety. The anxiety from before began to grip her once again. She held Rex closer. The creek was just up ahead, which meant she was halfway to Stephen's house; about a quarter mile from her house, about a quarter mile to go. By the time she reached the creek, her body was experiencing the first signs of the all-encompassing pain she had felt near Old Man Moody's mailbox. She breathed hard, trying to push it away. "Again?" I've got to get to Stephen's house! Mrs. Branton will know what to do!

Claire leapt over the small creek, and when she landed, a sharp stab entered her chest. A searing pain followed, straight up her spine to the base of her skull. "OH!" She fell, but threw Rex in front of her so as not to land on the little guy. When he hit the ground, he took off running, down the bank of the creek to where some stones set in the middle of the water. He jumped them one by one, crossing the stream in a flash, and darted back toward their house.

"Rex!" Claire called, but he didn't stop. "Rex..." She winced. "What is happening to me?" She lay on the bare shore and sobbed, not even caring that her flowery nightgown might be getting smeared with dirt. At least it hadn't rained recently, or she would be laying in mud. Something inside her pushed out a laugh. Here she was in some of the worst pain she had ever experienced in her life, for the second time in the last half-hour, and she was worried about getting her gown dirty because Mother would be mad. "Aaagh!" Claire shouted, and pushed herself to her knees.

Through the tall grass on the creek's bank, she saw the fence up ahead where she and Stephen would so often meet, both on and off horseback. That fence seemed miles away now. She sat back on her haunches and rested her hands on her knees. Why can't I go further? "Steeee-phennnn!" she shouted at the top of her lungs. Her shoulders lurched at her heavy breathing. "Hear me. Please," she gasped.

Claire stumbled forward and cried out as she landed on her face. Even to her own ears she sounded more like a pterodactyl from pre-history than a human girl. But she didn't care what she sounded like at that moment.

Stephen.

An image of the boy went through her mind one last time, and she passed out.

4

The House

Claire awoke on her tummy. She looked around. Where am I?

She heard crickets. Cicadas. She rolled on her left side and looked up to see two trees near her, dark against a deep blue sky. She rolled over all the way onto her back and let her head fall to the right. There, the orange clouds of sunset streaked to the horizon.

A dull aching filled her body. She sat up, and saw she was still on the north bank of the creek she was so familiar with. The one halfway to Stephen's house as the crow flies. Stephen! I must get to Stephen's house! She jumped up, then doubled over in pain. It felt as if she had been given the one-two punch in the gut by one of those heavyweight boxers her father enjoyed hearing fight on the radio. She fell to her knees, and crawled over to the stream. As she moved further south, the pain seemed to lessen, but only a little. Once at the water, she dipped her hand into it and brought the liquid to her lips. It tasted so good, so cool.

Claire sucked in a quick breath as the nausea grew worse. She closed her eyes and vomited into the water. When she opened her eyes again, the water where she had puked was brown and murky. She had not expected to see what was left of dinner, because she'd not had anything to eat all day, but she'd at least expected to see the usual yellowish bile of stomach-stuff floating about. But this resembled mud. Mud mixed with shredded, rotted wood or something. And the stench! It smelled like a dead animal! She pushed herself back into the tall grass, where the pain fully encompassed her once again. I have to get home. Maybe the pain will go away like it did last time, and I can try again tomorrow?

Claire tried to stand, but could not. She crawled back to the water's edge, and turned to look downstream, to ensure the rotting mud that had somehow come from her own stomach had floated away. She poured herself into the water. It came up to her elbows, and she remained there for a little while. The cool liquid and the babbling sound it made rushing over her was just so wonderful and relaxing.

Then her eyes snapped open. Had she fallen asleep again? She looked to the sky. It was still dusk. She crawled on, up onto the southern bank, and rolled onto her back. Her body ached, though it wasn't killing her like it had been moment ago. A hypothesis formed in her mind. She rolled over onto her belly and crawled on all fours through the deepening grass, toward her home. The pain began to subside, little by little. She crawled faster. Her headache was lessening. She got her feet underneath her finally, and started tramping through the grass in big steps. The pain stayed behind. She began to run. With every step, the pain fell further and further away. As she passed her favorite tree, the one she often sat under to read or to look up at the stars, she smiled, then began to laugh. She felt good again. Good as new. As if—

Her smile faded when she glanced up and saw her house. Every window was lit, and she could see inside. Her eyes bulged and her jaw fell open. Is that furniture in there? Curtains? How? They weren't there only an hour ago! Or was it two?

She navigated the meadow at a slower pace. She came to a stop a few feet from where the tall grass met her back yard. "I couldn't have been asleep for more than a few hours!" She ducked down in the grass lest she be seen, and looked toward the setting sun. It had been lunchtime when she first started off for the Branton house. So… six hours? Seven? By the look of the sky, it must be seven or eight P.M. now. Not long enough for someone to move in!

Claire listened for a moment and, upon hearing or seeing no one, she dashed to the screened-in porch and entered the mud room, a small space that separated the "dirty outside" from the fine proper of the rest of the house. The "workman's foyer" her mother called it. Boots stood along the walls that Claire didn't recognize. None belonged to either her father nor any of their stable hands. A warm glow drew her into the small hallway that separated the parlor—now to her right—and the grand stair and main foyer to her left. She entered the foyer. When she rounded the corner, the large space once again sported small furniture along the walls. To her left, the kitchen door was open. Claire marveled that it once again looked like a warm, inviting place to make a meal. She tiptoed inside.

The only thing familiar was the layout. The kitchen cabinets had been painted white, whereas only a few hours ago they sported the natural color of oak. A new table and chairs set where her family's once had, and containers and appliances lay on the counters, the new-style ones similar to those she had seen in the Sears catalogue that Mother had wanted so badly. But these looked really new.

She reached the narrow door leading down to the cellar, but she passed by it because her gaze was drawn to the formal dining room. All the amenities had returned, though nothing like she remembered. The tablecloth shone white and lacey in the light of the beautiful chandelier above, which hadn't changed. A three-pronged candelabra stood at the center of the table, boasting dark blue candles that still had white wicks, indicating they had never been lit. The walls were now a light blue. Not her favorite but at least the ugly wallpaper was gone! Perhaps painted over? A large hutch stood in one corner, full of sparkling white china, saucers and cups. What is going on?

A bump came from upstairs.

My room! Claire wasted no time. Through the long foyer and up the staircase. She arrived in her bedroom before even she realized it. A bed and two dressers now stood along the walls. Curtains donned the windows. But normal white ones, not the frilly kind she loved so. And blue drapes of a shade that were just a little too dark for her taste. The furniture was nice, though. Several dolls stood or set on newly installed shelves, all dressed differently and beautifully. None looked like those she had seen in catalogues or in stores, not even on her family's trip to New York two years ago. But how did all this stuff get here? And so quickly? Her head jerked to her right, to the wall her room shared with the bathroom. The panel. It was closed.

And latched.

Claire dropped to her knees and in a single movement, ripped the bolt out of the latch. She dug her nails into the wood, and with a renewed strength, yanked it with a ferocity she never knew she possessed. She opened the door on the first try. Ha! I guess I broke the paint seal the last time! She put one arm into the hole in the wall, careful not to bump her head on the valve like she had so often done when she was little. Her hand found the small wooden box, and her heart started beating again. She closed her eyes and breathed a long, deep breath, then felt more than saw someone standing in the doorway. Claire jerked her head over her shoulder.

There stood a young girl, probably eleven or twelve years old, Claire guessed, still as a statue. The girl's mouth was clamped tight, and it seemed her eyes had frozen wild. She seemed to stare right into Claire's very soul.

Claire didn't know why the girl's eyes had grown as big as they had, but it might have been because this little intruder had just discovered her secret hiding place! "Who are you?" she asked, not politely in the least. "What are you doing in my house?" And with that, Claire slammed the panel shut. She wanted the girl to know there was nothing in there she should trifle with.

The child yelped when the panel banged against the wall, and she tore off down the hallway.

Claire's brow furrowed and she eyed the panel with suspicion. Why did it shut so easily this time...?

The girl's voice rang out from somewhere down the hall. "MOMMM!"

Claire rolled her eyes. Great. Now everyone will know about my hiding place. Where can I put my jewelry box now?

"Mom! I saw her, I saw her, I saw her!"

Well that's an odd thing to say. What, do they actually know someone lives here and moved in anyway?

"Where, honey?" The distant voice was quiet, motherly.

"Upstairs in my room!"

Gotta move quickly. She yanked the door wide open and stared as she worked it back and forth on its hinges. Did I finally loosen it up or something? She shook her head and retrieved her precious, wooden box. She looked around the room. No, not in here. But where...?

The attic!

Claire padded into the hall and found the heavy string to the pull-down staircase tucked away in the ceiling. She jumped up to grab it, but missed. Oh! Why did Father keep it cinched so high up? But she knew the answer: to keep her from playing up there. But now I need to get up there, Dad! It's important! She had lost everything, she wasn't about to lose the only things she had left in this life to people she didn't know, even if it was merely a tiny collection of trinkets and memories. They were her trinkets and her memories! She jumped again, and missed once more. She tried again, and managed to get a finger on it. It swung to and fro. "Oh, why can't I reach it?"

"There!" The little girl's voice now floated up the stairs. "You heard her that time, right?"

Claire waited.

"Go get your father."

No time to lose now. She growled, and put all her heart into it. She jumped, and this time, found her target. She hung there for a moment by one arm, her bare feet dangling. This thing is heavier than I remember! She yanked down on it over and over again, and the narrow staircase creaked open, but only slightly. Claire dangled and spun.

"What?" said a man's voice from somewhere on the first floor. "That can't be, sweetheart. What have I told you about telling stories?"

"I'm not telling stories! Go see for yourself!"

"Well maybe I will!"

Uh oh.

Claire wished she could use her other hand, but she wasn't about to let go of the jewelry box, not even for a second. She tugged and grunted and jerked on the string, and with one long swoop, the stair creaked downward, dropping her to the floor with a thump.

The mother gasped. "I definitely heard something that time!"

"I told you!" shouted the girl, "it's her!"

"Nonsense!" bellowed the father. "I'll show you two how crazy you are!"

Claire scampered up the narrow stair, barely wide enough for one person. She set the box down on the attic floor, and in a panic, reached down and yanked the stair shut with a bang.

Silence followed.

Claire looked around at the small attic. Aside from a handful of new wooden crates, it was mostly empty now that her parents' extensive belongings had been removed. She had every nook and cranny in easy view, but she was only concerned with one. The daylight was almost gone, but the small, rectangular windows on three of the slanting walls gave her enough light to see by. She squinted at the wall boards near the floor.

There it is! She darted to a narrow board and gave it a yank. But like the panel in her room, it was fastened good and tight. But Father said the nails were just sitting in the holes! That's how he always got it out so easily! She tried once more. "Oh! Not again!" she yelled, and kicked it. It then fell away from the wall like it had simply been leaning there. "What in the world?" she said to the Universe. Claire heard footsteps, and the voices returned, wafting up from below. No time to ponder this new mystery. She crouched before the hole in the wall. But before she stuffed her jewelry box inside, she reached in there, just in case. The hole was as empty as she presumed it would be. Her father had forgotten his own daughter, but had of course remembered to remove the money he always kept stashed in the attic in case of a robbery. "They might get the safe in the study open, but they won't find this!" Claire remembered him boasting. What she wouldn't give for that wad of cash now, it would be her ticket to Baltimore!

The voices beneath the floorboards grew louder, and she could almost understand them. She tucked her small box of memories into the wall and gritted her teeth as she put every effort into replacing the board.

"It had to be the stair," said the mother. "What else could have made that loud of a bang?"

"Okay I get how it may have fallen down," asked the father, "but how could it have gone back up?"

"Ha! See?" exclaimed the little girl, "Momma and I aren't crazy!"

"No," the father said, "there's got to be a rational explanation."

A pause.

"Daddy, look!"

More footsteps.

"Did you open that panel, Bobbie? I told you that was for the water! You are never to—"

"I didn't open it! She did!"

"Don't you raise your voice to me, young lady!"

"But Daddy!"

"That's enough! Enough from both of you! Bobbie, to your room! Margie, a word."

Claire looked around the dim attic. What am I doing hiding up here like a scared animal? Look at me! And still in my bed clothes! This is my house, not theirs! Why am I the one hiding from them!? She stood and headed toward the stair, but paused. She didn't really want to leave the attic. In all truth, she was terrified, embarrassed, and completely unsure what would happen next. Would they help her? Help her get to Baltimore? Or would they go and get the police, and tell them there was an intruder in the house? But the police would help, right? That's what they do for innocent people. Old Man Moody and Mr. Branton would surely tell them who she was. And then they'd have to wire her parents to let them know she was safe, and her Father would have to wire money for a train ticket. Either way, she would get to Baltimore. She made her decision, and pushed on the stairs. Like the panel and the board, the stair wouldn't move. Dad blame it! I'm too light. I probably need a little more oompf, that's all. She tried again. No luck. Was the stair locked into place? She looked for a locking mechanism, but found none.

Wait a second. What if it was only meant to open from the other side? And that's why Father never closed it when he was up here! Claire fought off an emerging panic. *Am I trapped? No, of course not! Just wait for the people below to pull the stair down, silly!*

She waited. Nothing happened.

The voices were quiet now. *Not only quiet, but gone! Maybe I am trapped after all?* Her eyes scanned the large, dark space for another way down, and remembered the small, recessed square set into one wall. Her father had called it a "maintenance" door, which connected the sewing room to the attic. As she padded to it, her mind traced a path through the third story of the house that she would take once through the door. Thanks to her father's recent renovations, most of the third floor was no longer just attic space but now livable space. But not if you were tall, hence why her tall father rarely ventured past the second floor. Of the three bedrooms adjacent to the attic, Mother had turned one into a sewing room, one into a storage space for flotsam and jetsam and holiday decorations, and the third into a spare bedroom for guests like Aunt Beatrice, who always seemed to show up at the most inopportune time. Claire reached the little door and pushed on it. It didn't move. She pulled. Same result. She felt around in the near-dark for the latch, but found only smooth wood. And then it hit her.

The latch is on the other side of the door, Claire.

She shook her head. *Figures.* She put a finger to her mouth and thought for a moment. Her gaze rose until it reached nine small square windows high above. Through them shone a dim purple-orange light; the clouds reflecting the last rays of the setting sun. She cocked her head. Well, if there wasn't a way down that involved the inside of the house, then...

She started for the nearest set of squares, which were really less than a proper set of windows and more of a way to vent heat (when cracked open) and to allow light inside. "Don't worry, Claire," she said to herself, "if you fall, it's only a three-story drop. Plus a little more." She hopped up on a wooden shelf that probably wasn't meant to hold her weight, under the three eastern-facing window-like things. She worked the latch of one small, square glass frame, and after a short time, the window pushed open. She instantly regretted the decision. Either the wind had picked up in the last half-hour, or it was so windy because she was so high up now. She shivered in her nightgown as she tried to judge the width of the square with her slim shoulders. Pbbt! I've squirmed through plenty of cracks and crevices smaller than that!

She rested her chest on the window frame, and looked out upon the house and the farms beyond her yard. Toward her front right stood the conical spire that rose tall and majestic above her father's study, one floor below. Beyond it, to the east, she could see Old Man Moody's house. Only two windows were lit; the kitchen and an upstairs bedroom. Claire wondered if the thin man she saw earlier might be in that upstairs bedroom. No. That's the Moody's bedroom. Ever since Mrs. Moody passed on, Mr. Moody never shut that lamp off. Ever. Claire only knew this because her father had told her so. He'd been able to see the light from his study. He'd said the lamp was always on when he went to bed, and always on when he woke up.

"Why does he always leave it on, Father?" she had asked.

"Mr. Moody leaves it on for his wife," came the reply. "In case she ever comes back..."

Claire shivered at the memory of that, and did her best to flush it from her head. She poured herself out of the small square and onto the slanted roof. She was thankful for the rough shingles, for they held her blouse fast. She worked her way down to an outcropping where a horizontal peak made the roof of the sewing room. She straddled the crest, placed her hands on either thigh, and rested a moment while she worked out what to do next.

She looked to her left, to what she understood to be north, and could just make out the lights of the Branton house a half-mile away. If only she had made it there this afternoon! She would be warm and in proper clothes and even better, in the arms of the boy she loved. As long as Mrs. Branton would allow such things in her house, anyway. Probably not. No matter; instead she sat on a cold rooftop trying to find a way back inside her own home, which was now infested with people she had never even seen before!

She looked to her right, toward the front yard. The spire was mostly in the way but she could see the dirt road that passed directly in front of her home as it stretched for miles in either direction, east and west. She saw no horses, no buggies. Not a soul traveled the road right now, and Claire was thankful for that. A young girl in a nightgown up on a roof at dusk would surely draw quite a lot of public attention! If she were going to face this family, she would do it inside, and on her own terms. Not with an audience of townsfolk pointing and gossiping and giggling at the silly girl stuck on the roof!

Time to do this, before someone does happen by! She assumed all the proper windows to the sewing room beneath her were locked, and she didn't have anything with which to break one. Except for my hard head, of course, she thought with some amusement. Might as well see for sure, though. Nothing to lose.

Claire shimmied down one side of the peak feet-first, and stood on the guttering as she balanced herself against the slanted roof before her. She inched to the edge where the roof ended and took a deep breath. She placed a death-grip on the wood where it met the shingles and felt around with her right toe, until she found the windows' ledge. It wasn't hard to maneuver around to the small windows, only a little terrifying. She tried not to look down, but couldn't help herself. She gasped at how far away the grass appeared, and closed her eyes until the vertigo passed. She then realized she was holding her breath, and forced herself to breathe again. Get this over with, Claire! She opened her eyes and tried one of the windows. Locked. So were the other two. Naturally.

She turned her head. Only a few feet behind her, the spire marked the tallest point on the house, even taller than the wrought iron fence work at the top of the center crest. What that fence was for, beyond decoration, was something only the idiot builder could have told her. Could she work her way into one of the windows of the study? No, they're surely locked too. At least, her mother and father had always kept windows locked when they were shut, and there was no reason to expect these new people were anything out of the ordinary. There's nothing to stand on anyway. Could she shimmy down the side of the house somehow? She looked around for any footholds, but there were none. Not on this side of the house anyway. On the other side was a vine ladder. Stephen had often taken advantage of it to climb up to her bedroom. At the front of the house was her parents' balcony. Claire, you dolt, you picked the wrong side of the house!

Her only option was to go back up and come down another way. Shaking her head, she inched back over to the corner and, moving faster this time, swung around the edge and planted her foot on the guttering. Or at least she thought she had. Her breath caught in her throat and her fingers slipped from their purchase. She flailed, hyperventilating for air, grasping for wood, shingles, anything. Her hand slammed against the guttering as she fell, making a loud crack, but it didn't stop her.

She screamed all the way down.

Claire's back hit the ground first, followed by her skull. With the wind knocked out of her, she could only pant and whimper. Her back had to be broken. Everything had to be broken. She opened her eyes. At least they still worked!

She looked up at the heavens. It wasn't completely dark yet, but the stars were out, forming their constellations as best they could. She scanned the velvety purple for the Dippers. There they were, off to her right. Okay so that's north. Got my bearings again.

Her father, the self-proclaimed Premier Astronomer of King City, Missouri, had taught her that the final star in the tail of the Little Dipper was the North Star, named "Polaris", the one that never moves in the night sky. He told her that as long as she could find the Big Dipper, it would lead her to the Little Dipper, and then she could find Polaris easily. It would always tell her which way north was, and she would never be lost. She remembered that all her life. And beyond.

Directly in front of her, as she lay on her back, was the mighty Hercules, fighting the great dragon Draco. To her dismay, her favorite constellation, Orion the Hunter, was not visible in September from this lattitude. She turned her head to the left, then right, looking for the Moon. She couldn't find it. Good! A New Moon meant there would be less light for anyone to see her lying out in the yard in her nightgown!

She paused in her thoughts, and scrunched up her face. Something wasn't right. She turned her head back to the left. Then again to the right. Why doesn't that hurt? Shouldn't that hurt? She did the same thing again. Still no pain. Her brows furrowed, and she sat up on her elbows. Nothing. How is this possible? Falling three stories should rightly smart! Something didn't add up. The fall hadn't killed her, but surely it broke something! She moved her feet and wiggled her toes. No pain of any kind. Claire cocked her head. "So," she said out loud, "if I walk too far down the road, if I cross the creek to Stephen's house, I double over in agony. Fall off a roof, and I feel great. Well, that's a new one!"

She got to her feet and instinctively went to brush herself off, but found her nightgown as perfectly clean as when she'd gone to bed last night. Her chin doubled up at the mystery. No dirt? I should be filthy! She had crawled through the creek, lay on the bank, traipsed through the tall grass, shimmied around on the roof of her house, and not a single smear or smudge? Not a single blade of grass stuck to her? Not even specks of tar from the roof?

She studied her hands, touched her head. She was there, alright. Alive and well. "Something is definitely amiss!" she said aloud. She did her best to make head or tail of all these mysteries as she walked around to the screened-in porch. She figured the back door was the best chance of getting inside now, same way she had less than an hour ago. Sure enough, she was standing in the mud room before she knew it.

Light still radiated from the direction of the kitchen. "Okay Claire, let's claim our home!" She steeled herself, and marched into the short hall. To her right lay the parlor, to her left, the foyer. She turned left, rounded one more corner, and found herself at the foot of the grand stair, facing the front door at the other end of the long foyer. "Hello?" she called. No answer, and no sign of the new family that was currently trespassing in her home. She tried again. "Hellooo-ohhh."

She waited. Still no answer.

"Is anyone here?" she called out, then stood still and listened. Not a peep. Claire set her jaw. "Okay, where are you people?" Did I pass out again for a while, when I fell off the roof? Maybe they're all in bed and simply didn't turn out the lights?

Directly behind her, the elegant staircase wound up to the bedrooms, the bath, the sitting room, and the study. She turned and stomped up the stairs. She had rounded the landing and was halfway up the longer flight of stairs when she heard the front door open and close. There they are! She turned to head back down the stairs, but something made her stop and listen, out of view of the foyer or the door.

"I know we're not crazy, Alfred!" It was the mother again. "I'm certain even the neighbors heard that scream!"

"I know, dear, I heard it from the study. And what sounded like the guttering peeling away from the house."

"But what could it have been? An animal? A bird?"

"I don't know, Margaret, I guess so." He let loose a sigh. "At least I hope so. This house is starting to unnerve me."

"Starting to?"

Oh, it was just me! Claire rolled her eyes. It's time to get this over with. And I'll finally be able to get some decent clothes and a ticket out of here! She stood up straight, ran her fingers through her unruly mess of red hair, and ran down the stairs. She stopped on the landing when she saw no one in the foyer. Where did they go? Ugh. The kitchen, probably. It was the only room where light peeked around the edges of the now closed door. Claire marched down the smaller flight, took a deep breath, and burst into the kitchen to proclaim greetings and to claim her property. But no one was there, either.

Claire looked over her shoulder, to make sure no one had snuck around behind her from the dining room, or one of the rooms on the other side of the foyer. But no one had. Her brow furrowed, and she padded through the kitchen to the dining room. It was as devoid of life as it had been earlier. "Hello?" she called.

No answer.

She stomped across the foyer to the living room. Empty. The parlor. Also empty. And no replacement pool table as of yet. "Hello!"

Still nothing.

Claire's blood boiled. "I know you're here!" she shouted. "I just heard you talking! Stop playing games! This is my house! You're not going to do this to me in my own home! Now show yourselves!" She waited. Nothing. "Aaargh!" she shouted. "How did you people sneak past me?"

Claire flew up the staircase. When she reached the hallway at the top of the stairs, she looked both directions. All the doors were open, and all the lights were lit in all the rooms. She heard a clinking sound straight ahead of her, coming from the master bedroom.

She paused again. Polite manners had been drilled into Claire from the moment she came into this world, or at least as long as she could remember. She knew better than to barge into someone else's bedroom! But she had also heard her father say, "Desperate times call for desperate measures!" She turned her hands into fists, mashed her lips together, and stomped into what was once her parents' bedroom.

No one greeted her. No one demanded to know what she might be doing there. But the room... it was gorgeous! Claire had never seen a bed like the one that towered before her now. It was at least twice the size of her parents' old bed. And the dressers and vanity! The mahogany wood looked flawless. The ornate carvings were of the highest craftsmanship. The walls sported the prettiest pastel pattern she could imagine. A portrait of a regal man hung on the wall, painted in a style she didn't recognize. It looked—what was that word she had heard used? "Progressive." The entire room took her breath away. "Wow," she said aloud. The vanity had one of the largest mirrors Claire had ever seen. When she stepped in front of it, she noticed the sunburn she had gotten from riding so long yesterday had gotten worse. Not only were her nose and forehead peeling, but her cheeks as well. And her skin looked almost ashen! She looked down at herself, and her breath caught in her throat. Her arms were their normal creamy white, with a hint of pink. There was no peeling, no sunburn. Claire looked up, at her reflection again. In the mirror, ashen, but cream in real life. She touched her face as she stared at herself in the looking glass. Where her skin peeled before her eyes, she felt no detached skin. Her forehead and cheeks felt smooth as silk, as they always had. Her lips pursed. "What in all that is holy—?"

"Do you feel that?" came a feminine voice from somewhere off to her right.

Claire jerked her head in that direction. Was the mother in the walk-in closet? She started forward, toward the closed door.

"Yes, I feel it!" That was the father. His voice came from right behind her.

She spun 'round, but saw no one. But he seemed so close! Why couldn't she see him?

"It's like a... a cold, winter breeze, but without any wind," he went on to say. "Like a chill just... hovering in the air."

"Where are you?" Claire asked. "I can hear you, but—"

"Oh my Lord!" said the mother. "It's very cold right here!"

Her voice. Claire swallowed hard. It was right in her ear. And her right arm and shoulder grew warm, like the sun shone directly on her skin there.

"Yes," said the father, now just as close. "Someone or something is here..."

"Alfred, stop, you're scaring me."

"Margaret, go check on Roberta."

"I'm right here," said a young voice.

Claire recognized it. She spun around, and stared right into the eyes of Bobbie, the little blonde girl she'd seen earlier.

Bobbie stared directly at her, and swallowed before speaking again. "You can't see her, can you?"

"See who, sweetheart?"

"The red-haired girl in the flowery nightgown with the blood stain," Bobbie replied in a shaky voice. "She's standing right in front of you both."

Claire furrowed her brow. Blood stain? She looked down. Sure enough, a dark red stain had appeared in the middle of her chest. That wasn't there before! The fall. The fall must have done it! Claire felt her chest. It didn't hurt, but for that much blood, there must surely be a rib jutting out of her skin or something! She felt around on top of the gown, but found nothing out of the ordinary. Perhaps it wasn't her blood? But if not her own, then whose? Did I land on an animal?

Wait. What's that?

She had found something. Her fingers came across a small line, a cut in her skin. With both hands she pulled the top of her gown a few inches from her body and peered downward. Just off center, in her left breast, she found a small slit. She guessed it was an inch wide. It was caked with blood.

"Tell us what you see, honey," said the father.

"Well," the girl said, whetting her lips, "she's now clutching her chest. And by the look on her face... It's like she didn't know the blood was there before I said something."

Claire felt tears welling up.

"I'm right, aren't I?" the girl asked Claire.

"You say she's got red hair?" asked the mother. "Like the girl who... who we were told died in this house?"

Bobbie nodded. "The girl who was murdered, you mean."

Murdered! Claire shook her head. This was all too confusing. She looked around the room. She only saw the girl, but she could hear the voices of the parents as plain as day. Surely they weren't... ghosts!?

"I think she's scared," the blonde girl said, now stepping fully into the room. "Miss? Are you scared?"

Claire turned back to her. She backed away at the girl's approach. "I'm..." She could barely speak. "I'm..."

The father's disembodied voice rang in her ears. "Sweetheart, what's she doing now?"

Bobbie stopped a few feet from Claire and held up a palm, then put a finger to her lips with her other hand. "Shhh, she's trying to say something."

Claire shook her head. "I'm... Am I dead?"

Bobbie nodded, tears now forming in her eyes. "I think so," she whispered.

It would explain so much, Claire thought. Why the fall didn't hurt me. Why my gown didn't get dirty.

Why no one answered me when I called out to them, all day long. Why Rex growled and seemed so terrified of me.

Why my parents left me.

"But..." Claire stammered. "Murder!?"

"Yes," Bobbie said. "That's what we were told."

A thousand questions flooded Claire's mind. "But by whom? How? When?"

"Six years ago. They said the neighbor boy did it."

Claire's eyebrows worked up and down. "Neighbor boy?" She thought about everyone who lived around her. Old Man Moody. Abraham Moody. The Johansens in the newer house to the west. No, they only had daughters. The Hayward's son, across from the Johansens, was killed in the Civil War. The only neighbor left—

No.

Claire shook her head, slow at first, then more violently. No. No, it couldn't have been! "Stephen?" Claire asked.

The little girl said nothing.

Claire began to hyperventilate. "No, not Stephen. He would never hurt me! He said so!" Then she remembered his quickness to anger. His violent temper. How his mood and attitude toward her had changed after she told him they had to move. Until her last day, and then he had been back to his happy-go-lucky self again. The boy she'd fallen in love with. "He even visited me on my last night here! He climbed up the ivy ladder to my window, like he did on many occasions when Mother and Father were asleep." She smiled. "I was so happy to see

him, to spend one last night in his arms! He said...
what did he say?" Claire racked her brain to
remember. "He said he had found a way so that I
could stay. And we would be together forever. He
said he had gotten the idea from William..."

A single tear made its way down the girl's cheek.
"William... Shakespeare?"

It hit Claire like a kick from a horse. Her and
Stephen's families didn't approve of them seeing
one another. Their fathers hated each other. Fights
had ensued. Threats. Her father often promised her
mother, if "that ruffian ever touches Claire, there
will be blood!" Stephen is Romeo. I am Juliet. And
Romeo and Juliet, they—

A searing ache shot through Claire's chest, and she
doubled over and cried out, clutching the place
where Stephen had slipped the knife between her
ribs and into her heart. Her vision blurred as her
eyes filled with tears. Her hands went to the sides of
her head and she pulled hard at her hair. She spun
around, her lip quivering as the realization overtook
her. She inhaled as deeply as she could, threw her
head back, and wailed. "Noooo!"

Bobbie's palms smashed against her ears.

Margaret, the mother, screamed.

"Roberta!" shouted the girl's father.

Movement appeared in Claire's vision. She ceased
her wailing and gasped. She could see them now.
The parents! But only the slightest whisper of an
outline, as if they were ghosts themselves.

Alfred, the father, reached out to Bobbie. "Come
on, we're leaving!"

They heard me cry out just then! And they heard me scream when I fell, too!

"Daddy, it's okay!" The little girl fought against the outline of a man who was dragging her backwards against her will. "Daddy! Mommy! It's okay! I don't think she's going to hurt us!"

"I'm not giving her the chance!" her father shouted. "Now hurry! Leave everything! Get to the carriage! We'll send for our things!"

"No!" Claire cried. "Wait! Please! I don't know what to do now! I don't know how to be a—Oh!" Her hand went to her mouth. Oh my Lord! The thin man in Old Man Moody's house! He must have been a ghost too! She whirled around and peered through the black glass behind her, half expecting to see him right outside on the balcony in the moonlight, waiting for her. She backed away from the windows.

"Daddy, stop! She's just scared! She only now found out she's dead!"

"Listen to what you're saying, Bobbie! We're leaving!"

"No! Daddy, please wait!" About half way down the long flight leading to the only landing on the grand staircase, the girl fought off her father's grip. "I can see her!" she said, pointing upward. "She's not coming after us! She's terrified! She's just a young girl like me! Why can't you see her?"

"I don't know and I don't rightly care at the moment!" shouted the father from the first floor. "And it absolutely disturbs me that you can! Which is precisely why we're leaving, this house is haunted! Now get down here!"

Bobbie stomped her foot. "But we knew it was haunted before we even moved in!"

"It was all silly superstition before! Now it's not!" The man's voice sounded more distant now, like he was at the other end of the foyer. "Now come, Roberta! No more lip! Let's go!"

Bobbie turned and ran back up.

Claire met her at the top of the stairs. The father's voice, softer now, wafted up to her ears. "Wait here, Margaret. I'll go get the carriage from the barn."

"Hurry, Alfred!" the mother pleaded.

"And get that girl to come along!"

"Roberta!" she called. "Come along, now!"

"I'm sorry," the blonde girl said in a gentle voice to Claire, ignoring her mother. "I didn't know you didn't know."

Claire wiped tears from her eyes. "I think I did. I simply couldn't make myself believe it. Thank you. Thank you for telling me."

The girl gave her a tight grin. "I'm sorry I have to leave now. I think we might have been friends."

This made Claire smile from ear to ear.

"I can tell you were really pretty. Or, I mean, are really pretty. Despite all the... um..." Here she put her hand to her forehead, then her cheeks.

Claire touched her face, but still felt nothing unusual. She looked away, remembering what she had seen in the mirror.

"I'm sorry about what happened to you. I would like to help you, but my father—"

"I understand," said Claire.

The girl nodded. "Are you going to be okay?"

Claire looked back at her and tried to smile. But then she closed her eyes and shook her head, and her lip started quivering again. She wrapped her arms around herself for comfort.

"Roberta!" called her mother once more. "Your father will be back any minute with the carriage! Don't make him come up there and get you!"

Bobbie chuckled. "Don't worry. I don't think he would even if he had to."

Claire coughed, a small laugh and a small cry bursting forth at the same time.

"Would you tell me your name?" the little girl asked. "You don't have to if you don't want to. I just wanted to know who you were. I mean, who you are. I'm Bobbie."

Claire tilted her head in awe at this amazing young person, who'd overcome her own fear to help a stranger in need. Who'd helped make sense of a topsy-turvy situation, the result of a tragedy, a heinous crime that made Claire the Alice of her own Wonderland. "My name is Claire. Claire Harvey."

Bobbie smiled. "Nice to meet you, Claire. I hope you find peace here. I hope you find your way to Heaven someday."

Tears spilled over from Claire's eyes. "Thank you, Bobbie."

The sound of clopping hooves wafted up the stairs. Roberta turned and headed down the grand staircase. At the landing, she paused. She looked up, held up her hand, and gave the tiniest of waves.

Claire returned the gesture to her new friend.

A horse neighed, and Alfred's voice could be heard once again. "Roberta! We're leavinnng!"

The little blonde girl glanced back up at Claire one last time and mouthed, "Bye." She then bolted down the smaller flight of stairs and out of sight.

Claire listened as the girl's footsteps faded, the front door closed, and the new family was gone.

5

Departure

"I wish I could help you pack," Claire said, standing in the doorway with her arms crossed.

Max looked up from the suitcase on his bed. He seemed startled. "No you don't."

His voice is so deep now. I'll never get used to it this way. She looked down and adjusted her arms so they better covered the ugly blood stain on her otherwise beautiful nightgown.

"I was starting to think you weren't going to say goodbye."

"Well that's silly," replied Claire. "Why would you think that?" Before he could answer, she changed the subject. "So did Sophie's rejection letter come in the mail yet?"

"Why do you think it would be a rejection letter?"

Claire tilted her head sideways. "It's your nasty sister we're talking about here. She's been trying to get into college for two full years now. "

"You're the only one who thinks of her like that."

"She's nasty to me."

"You're right, it was another rejection. But she didn't have a tutor like I did."

Claire twisted her face into the most evil smile she could muster. "Ha! I'll still have someone to haunt."

"Oh, Claire, leave her alone."

"What? Why would I do that?"

"Haven't you tortured her enough for the last twenty years?"

"Hey it's not my fault she's terrified of me. You weren't. So why was she?"

Her student, now older than she in apparent age, shrugged his manly shoulders.

Claire dropped her hands to her sides and moped into his room, the room that used to be hers, the room she had been murdered in. "If she hadn't screamed and panicked every single time she laid eyes on me, from the day she was born, I might have tried harder to have some kind of relationship with her."

As Max collected small items to take with him, Claire's gaze wandered to the small television on the dresser. Some newscaster was on, talking about how a meteorite believed to be from Mars might contain a fossil, indicating microscopic life may have once thrived on the Red Planet. Claire scoffed.

"What?" asked Max.

"My father might have believed that silliness," she said, motioning to the T.V., "but they're not fooling me! He was such a sucker when it came to anything about outer space!"

Max stopped packing for a moment. "You look different today, you know that? Oh! No ponytail!"

"Yeah, I thought I'd change things up a bit. I've had my hair up in that ponytail since, oh, not long after you were born. You don't remember, but when you were a baby you used to pull my hair all the time. I got so tired of it! So I put it up and never let it down again."

"Sorry."

"Oh, it's okay. I kind of forgot about all that, to be honest." She played with the hair pin she had taken out of her hair only a few minutes ago. She hoped it never broke, because the chances of acquiring a new one were slim. She had tried to steal one of Sophie's elastic hair bands a few years back, but it was like carrying around a cinder block, so she went back to the pin she found stashed in her jewelry box at the time of her death. "At least you didn't throw every toy in reach at my face like your jitterbug sister did. She would pull my hair, too, only she wouldn't let go. Oh, that nasty little monster!" Claire physically shrugged off the bad memory. "Anyway, now that you're moving away and starting a new chapter in your life, I decided I should, too. So, I figured it was time to let it back down like I always had it when I rode at top speed across the countryside on my mighty Velvet!" She lowered her voice. "When my mother wasn't dictating my every move, that is."

"Yeah I just..." Max began, "I guess I just never knew there was so much of it!"

Claire tossed her head from side to side, tussling her red mane further.

"You look so... different."

Claire went fishing. "Different bad, or different good?" She gave him a long stare, one she was sure he would look away from, and he did after a few seconds. But their eyes had met long enough. She'd gotten her message across.

He seemed to think about things before answering. "Different good," he said, then went back to packing.

Claire studied him. He was avoiding her stare, pulling away again. He had done so only two other times since he had turned sixteen, when Claire began to tease and flirt to see where things might go. Each time was when he'd tried dating. She took care of both of those problems in short order, as soon as she decided she liked neither girl. Which was pretty much the moment she first laid eyes on them. This time, however, was different. There wasn't another girl involved. She suspected he was pulling away because he was leaving, and he didn't want to make it harder than it already was. She understood that.

Or so she told herself.

But really, what did she expect? They could barely hold hands, let alone—

"I'm sorry we never kept horses on the property, Claire," Max blurted, interrupting her thoughts. "I know you would have loved to go riding again. Not sure the horses would have allowed it, though. And, you know, it's the nineties, after all."

"People ride horses still. I see them on T.V.," she said, and glanced back at the television. The newscaster was now going on about the closing ceremonies of the Olympic Summer Games.

"You know what I mean. If people have them it's mainly just for sport now, for fun. Who can afford fun like that?"

"You can afford a fancy car. And a very expensive college."

"The scholarship and the college fund my father set up ages ago is paying for college. And the car isn't fancy. What would you know? You've never even ridden in a car!"

"I've seen them drive by!" Claire retorted. "And I've seen them in the movies. I know when one's fancy and when one's not. BMWs are fancy!"

"It's twelve years old. Those are cheap. Besides, we have to have cars nowadays; they're our horses now. I can't exactly go to work on a real horse!"

"Why not?"

Now it was Max's turn to cock his head sideways.

"Okay, okay." Claire sat down at Max's old study desk. There wasn't much space left for textbooks now that a big machine set on it. Max called it a "computer." It now helped him with his homework more than she did. "But you know, I'm sure Traci Underhill would have had a full-on heart attack of looove if you picked her up on a horse!"

Max's eyes locked on hers.

"Well she would have."

"Guess I'll never know now, will I?"

"Hey, I didn't so much as let an ethereal breeze blow by her the last two or three times you brought her over. I stayed tucked away, just like you asked me to. Her breaking up with you wasn't my fault."

"It wasn't?" Max stuffed a t-shirt into his suitcase. "Could have fooled me."

"If she hadn't have been snooping around in the first place, she never would have found me."

He haphazardly folded a dress shirt.

Claire's gaze fell upon the closet door in the corner. "I wonder what she was looking for in there, anyway?"

"Why were you hiding in there?"

"Where else was I supposed to hide without you seeing me?"

"Oh, I don't know, the kitchen, the living room, the sitting room, the parlor, the study? Outside? Pretty much anywhere but here?" he shouted, and threw the now crumpled shirt into his suitcase, then reached for the last one lying on his bed.

"Hmm." Claire put a finger to her mouth. "Yes, I could have just hovered outside the window..."

"You're missing the whole point!"

She giggled.

"All I wanted was just a little privacy!"

She scoffed. "That's why I was in the closet, silly!"

"Aaargh!"

It's so easy to get under his skin. "Oh Max, I'm only teasing."

"You know," Max said, turning toward her, "you could have just made yourself invisible to everyone, and not even I would have ever known you were there, let alone her! And maybe, just maybe—"

"Where's the fun in that?" Claire interrupted.

He threw the last shirt into the suitcase as if he was pitching a fast ball.

"Oh, come on, Max, she was way too into herself anyway. Not to mention nosy. And pushy. And superstitious."

Max put a hand on his forehead. "Superstitious? Are you kidding?"

Claire leaned forward in the chair. "You're welcome."

Max threw his hands in the air, and crossed the room to his dresser. He pulled out three pairs of jeans, then returned to the bed.

"Okaaay, I'm sorry. Forgive me?"

"I'll think about it."

"You already have. But you know what? I've been thinking..." She crossed her legs and leaned back. "Why should I care if you go on dates with the living? I've got plenty of ghostly gentlemen suitors just dying to court me!" She smiled. "Pun intended."

Max chuckled. "Good one."

"Thank you."

Max folded his jeans with all the skill of someone who had barely graduated from folding shirts.

Claire giggled and rolled her eyes. "Nice job."

"Like you could do better."

"I could!" Her voice dropped. "If I could lift them."

"Exactly." A silence fell between them, but only for a few seconds. "Tell me, what ghostly gentlemen might you be referring to, Miss Claire? The phantom of the movie theater in town?"

"Like I can get to town," she muttered.

"Maybe the scary thin man from down the street?"

"No!" Claire shouted, and shivered. "Thankfully I haven't seen him in a good fifty years. Hopefully he's moved on or found the way out." She let out a long breath. "Unlike I've been able to do."

Max dropped the jeans into his suitcase. "I'm going to find a way to get you out of here, Claire. I promised you a long time ago I would. I meant it back then, and I mean it even more now."

"I know you do, Max. I still don't think science is the answer, but you're a lot smarter than me when it comes to such things."

"Like you're not smart in science."

"You know I'm not."

"Only because the things we know today weren't discovered by the time you were..." he caught himself and continued, "by 1899! Or you'd be a genius in that, too. You taught me everything I know about science and mathematics!"

"You give me far too much credit! I could only help you until eighth grade, silly. After that you started teaching me things."

"Maybe, but you have this knack for grasping things so quickly! I've never been able to match it. As soon as you hear something, you got it, you understand it, and you fly intellectual circles around me!"

"Oh, Max, stop."

"It's true, and you know it. I have to study my butt off in every subject, but for you... it's not fair. It really isn't."

Claire feigned a school-girl giggle. "Oh go on." She waited, but he didn't say more. "No, I mean go on, go on!"

Max laughed.

I love it when he laughs.

He walked over and knelt in front of her at the desk, and picked up her hands in his, as best he could.

Claire looked down at their clasped fingers. She closed her eyes. "Your hands are always so hot." Her eyes opened and she stared into his, only inches away now. "I'm sorry it's always been the opposite with me, like cuddling a giant block of ice."

Max shook his head. "You know I've never minded. Okay, well, at first I might have, but I got used to it. And now look! Any time I sleep somewhere else, I kick the covers off because I'm too hot! Because you're not lying there next to me."

Claire smiled and caressed his face with a stray finger. She wanted to kiss him, she wanted to give him a reason to stay. But she knew she shouldn't, and not only because it might have made it more difficult for him to go. It was the Universe. Would it allow such a thing as an intimate physical relationship between the dead and the living? Would God? She learned of something called the "kiss of death" in an old movie, and never forgot it. Max always thought she was being silly, but she refused to take chances. So it was for these reasons they had only held hands, and she would snuggle with him as he slept. Sort of; Claire would lay next to him on top of the covers because for one thing, the blanket kept him warm from her direct touch, and for another, she couldn't get under the blanket anyway. And she never exactly slept, not inside the house. She couldn't. The only place she could sleep seemed to be out in the meadow.

"I am really going to miss the coolness of your touch," Max went on to say. "It's really not that cold. Not unless you get upset. Or angry."

Claire thought of the times she had gotten angry with Max. After she'd promised him so many times she never would. But it was few and far between when it did happen. She counted all of two times.

There was the time when Max turned twelve and told her he was getting too old to have "an imaginary friend." She'd reminded him she wasn't imaginary, but since she had never allowed any of his friends to see her, she might as well have been. But that turned out to be easy to fix. Dejected, she went out into the meadow behind the house and took a nap. When she awoke some months later and was reunited with Max, he'd never wanted her to leave again. Claire decided she was lucky only a few months had passed, and not years. She swore she would never do that again while Max was still alive. Or at least living in her old house.

Then there was the first time he brought a girl to the house, when he was sixteen. Claire surprised herself with her own jealousy. It didn't go well. It would be a full year before he tried again with another young victim, the unfortunate Miss Underhill. After Claire scared her off, Max finally took the hint, and hadn't dated since.

No. It was three times I've gotten upset with him. The third time being right this very minute! How dare him! How dare he even consider leaving me for school! He can still go to school and not leave me! "Why do you have to go away? There are plenty of good colleges near here, I saw the commercials!" Claire let go of his hand and counted off on her fingers. "There's Missouri Western State University in Saint Joseph, it's only twenty-five miles away, and I know your fancy cars can go that far super quick! There's Norwest Missouri State—"

"They don't have what I want to study," Max interrupted.

She pressed her lips together.

"To keep my promise to you, I have to go to MIT. Or at least start there. We talked about this, Claire."

She looked away. "I know." He's only going away so he can help me. If it wasn't for me being stuck in this stupid house, he wouldn't have to go to a school so far away. If I wasn't stuck in this stupid house, he could go to whatever school he wanted and it wouldn't matter, because I could go with him! What did Max say that was? A "Catch-22"? "You're right," she said.

"Of course I'm right."

"No, I meant you were right when you said that I don't wish I could help you pack. In fact, I actually considered not saying goodbye."

"Why would you not want to bid me farewell and good luck and see me off?"

"Well," she mumbled, "I'm not very good with farewells. They've just happened so much in my life, and unfortunately, they're usually permanent."

"Oh, Claire, don't be silly," Max said, taking her hands in his once again, "I'll be back at Christmas. And then I'll probably come back in the summertime. For a while."

"You'll probably come back?" She squinted one eye.

"I will," he corrected. "I will come back."

"For a while...?"

"Don't look at me like that. Of course I'll come back."

She puckered her lips off to one side of her face. She desperately wanted to believe him, but the truth was, she didn't. "For how long?"

"Well, you know... I mean..." he stammered, "I don't know exactly how long—"

"You'll have the whole summer off, right? Like you did in high school?"

"Yeah, sure."

"So you'll be home for three months."

"Um, yeah, maybe."

"What do you mean 'maybe'?"

"Maybe," he said in a defiant tone.

"Why wouldn't you?"

He shrugged and looked down at their clasped hands. "I don't know. I might get a job or something."

"You could get a job here. In King City."

He didn't reply.

"You can get your old job back at the Dairy Hut!"

"Claire..."

"Or maybe at the movie theater! Oh, how I always wanted to go to a movie theater! Not that I could even if you got a job there, but—"

"I might meet somebody, okay?"

Claire's brow furrowed. There it is. The real reason. "But, you have somebody. Me."

"Claire," Max said with a heavy sigh, "we've been over this."

"Yes, we have. And I think I've done very well not to get angry with you about it, haven't I?"

"Why would you get angry? There's nothing anyone can do about it. Not right now, anyway."

"Stay! Please."

"Claire, I can't stay. I have to go. I have to learn everything I can about physics and meta-physics and engineering and paranormal... things... if there even is such a way to study that."

"What if there isn't a way out? What if God's punishing me for something and there's nothing you can do? Then I'll have lost you for nothing!"

"You won't lose me."

"If you meet someone else, I will!"

"Claire!"

She turned away.

"Um, Claire?" Max pleaded. "My hands... They're starting to freeze."

She looked down and noticed the grip she had on him. To her, his hands felt like they were burning up; the difference in temperature between she and Max had increased drastically. She relaxed, and let go.

"Thank you," he said, breathing on his hands and stuffing them under his armpits.

"I'm sorry," she said. "You know I can't help it. I'm just... I'm going to miss you."

"I know. I'm going to miss you, too."

"It's only natural I feel this way."

Max cleared his throat. "Is it?"

She stared at him.

"I mean, is it really natural?" he asked. "Claire, I love you, you know that. I probably always have and always will. And I know you love me. You've told me more times than I can count! But Claire... my darling Claire..."

She narrowed her eyes and waited for him to say it.

His voice once again fell to a whisper. "You're a ghost."

She gave him a look that could kill—as she'd heard say, but it never did—then turned away.

"Now, Claire, please don't... Let's not do this again."

"Do what again?"

He let out a deep breath but said nothing.

She stood from the desk and walked over to the window. She crossed her arms and peered out at the streetlights and trees that lined Hollow Street, or what some of the old folks—herself included on occasion—still called "Old Hollow Road." She stood on the rug, careful to avoid standing directly on the dark stain on the hardwood floor no one wanted to talk about. The ethereal blood no one could remove.

"Claire, I'm going to grow old," Max said from the bed behind her. "You're not. I have to live my life, just like you... well, like you would have, had you been given the chance."

"But I wasn't given the chance, was I?" she said, whirling around to face him, her fists shaking. "My life was taken from me!" She guessed her skin was peeling before his eyes; his expression told her so every time she became angry. It was nothing she could help when her emotions got the best of her, she simply lost her focus. The air around her nearly froze, and she reverted to what she would have looked like in the grave. "It wasn't fair. I never got the chance to go to college! To get married! To have a family! To grow old with someone!"

"Claire, please stop!" Max pleaded, looking away. "I can't stand it when you turn like that!"

"Turn? Like what? Into a ghost? A real ghost? A demon?" She rose into the air above him, her flowery, bloody gown blowing in a wind that originated from God-knows-where. The room darkened, and a black fog arose from where she'd stood only a moment ago. She felt the skin on her face melt away, and bared teeth that yellowed in seconds. Her bony fingers reached out and touched him.

Max cried out as his skin froze on contact. "Claire!" He fell to the floor. "Stop! Please stop!"

Her jaw extended all the way to her exposed ribcage, and she let a shrill cry fill the entire house.

His hands pressed against his ears. "Claire! I mean it!" He cowered, and seemed to want to crawl under his bed.

She hovered closer, grabbing him with both hands now, her mouth a rotted, gaping maw that could devour him if she so chose.

He raised his hands before his face, and began to cry. "Why are you doing this to me, Claire? Why do you enjoy torturing people? People you say you love! Why, Claire? Why!?"

His cries and words snapped Claire out of her demon state. He's right. Oh, my Lord, what am I doing? She released the shivering man below her, who had become as small as that little boy she'd used to tutor so often. She floated back, giving him space. What's gotten into me? She blinked, and as fast as the wind and darkness had come, it ceased, and light returned to the room. Claire's skin re-formed around her bones, and her long, red mop grew back to its normal length. Her feet touched the ground, and she rushed over to where the love of her death lay on the floor. "Oh, Max!"

He yelped at her touch and jerked away.

Oh no! What have I done? "Max! Max, I'm so sorry! I don't know what came over me!"

His eyes. His eyes were so wild. His pupils bored into hers under heavy brows, unwavering. He gasped for air as if he had just run a marathon. He clenched his teeth between open, twisted lips. His jaw trembled and his body shook, like he had been pulled from an icy lake.

"Max, that will never happen again! Never, ever, ever!"

"Damn right it won't!" he blurted between gasps. He inched his way around her, still hugging the floor. "Max, don't look at me like that! Please! I'm so, so sorry!"

"Don't touch me!"

She backed away and gave him some space. She yearned to cover him with the blanket he had been so cozy under mere hours ago, but it would be nothing but a ten-ton piece of lead to her. Claire turned back to see Max bounding to his feet and diving for his suitcase, which he slammed shut and latched. She blinked herself across the room, and now blocked the door.

He yelped when he nearly ran into her. His shoulders slumped, he closed his eyes, and put one hand on his heart. His other hand clutched his suitcase and jacket so tightly his knuckles turned white. He took a deep breath, let it out slow, and when he opened his eyes, he seemed a bit more calm. But his voice was still shaky. "Get out of my way."

"Max, please don't leave like this."

He shook his head. "You may be able to play ghastly demon girl to my sister every time you take a notion, Claire, but you're not doing it to me and getting away with it. You've never taken it that far before. Not even close! Oh my God, Claire! I don't remember ever being that scared before in my whole life! Look at me! I'm shaking!"

She grabbed his hand and pulled it to her chest to steady it. He tried to pull away but she held his hand against her, as gently as she could manage. "No, Max, no! Please." His hands were on fire, surely due to his extreme emotion, and they jittered so.

He turned his head.

"Max, look at me."

"I can't."

"Please look at me?" Her vision became blurry. "Max, please."

He glimpsed in her direction, but timid, like a terrified animal.

She stared deep into his big brown eyes, and spoke deliberately. "I will never, ever, ever—not in a million years—ever do that to do you again."

"Not in a million years, huh?"

She shook her head. "Not in a billion."

"Well, Claire, I don't have a billion years like you might have. I only have sixty or seventy more, and that's if I'm lucky. And I don't have time to be spending the short years I have remaining on this Earth in this house, with someone who I can't trust not to take my very soul."

A tear ran down her cheek.

"That's what you did to me just now," Max whispered. "I honestly thought you were about to drag me to Hell. Not kill me. Not slice me to shreds and turn this whole room red with my blood. But rip my immortal soul right out of my body and send me straight to the fiery pit of eternity. Where all the other demons—who look just like you did a moment ago—would be waiting to torture me to the end of time for my sins."

She realized her mouth had fallen open. She shut it.

"Yeah. That's what it was like, Claire. You should have seen yourself!" He shook his head. "I never want to see anything like that again as long as I live!"

"You won't!"

"I will, Claire. I will see it every time I close my eyes."

She held her breath.

"Every time I close my eyes," he repeated. He yanked his hand away and pushed by her.

She gasped as he did so. She turned around to call out to him, but her throat was constricted, and her voice wouldn't work.

Max paused at the top of the grand stair, and dropped his head a moment. He then turned and stared her down from the corner of his eye. "Bye, Claire. I don't know if I'll be back."

She put one hand on her mouth and one on her belly. It ached like it did that first day she'd awoken on the cold, hardwood floor over a hundred years ago.

"If you really do care about me, if you ever did actually love me like you always said you did, you'll do something for me."

She could barely see him through her tears.

"I know you can make yourself invisible to everyone, whether they are believers or not. I want you to make yourself invisible again. But this time completely. I don't want Sophie seeing you anymore, not ever again. I don't want Mom to call and tell me she finally has proof there's a ghost in the house. Dad, well, you guys could never see each other anyway, so I'm not worried about him."

"And you?" she burst out, both her hands on her stomach now.

Max looked away. When he looked up again, the light from the window high over the staircase glinted off the tears that filled his eyes. "I don't... I don't know how I feel right now."

Her hand went to her mouth and she cried silently into it.

"I've gotta go."

"Max!"

He disappeared down the stairs.

"Max!" she cried. Her shrill voice resonated through every board in that old house on Hollow Street. The entire family must have heard her—possibly even Max's father for the first time in his life—but she didn't care.

Claire doubled over on the floor, her stomach in knots. It wasn't as bad as the pain that crippled her whenever she would venture too far from the house, but nearly so. She was unable to move. Unable to do anything but sob into her hands.

6

Return

"Claire?"

The voice came from a distance, as if in a dream.

"Claire!"

She awoke with a start in the tall grass. She sat up and looked around for the speaker, but she was alone. "Rex? Where do you disappear to, you little mutt?"

Only crickets and cicadas answered her.

"Oh you spoiled little beagle! Ever since you died you've been as bad as a darned cat!" She looked all around her and listened for his bell. It was easier now that the crickets' chirping had died away; an angry ghost will do that to Nature. But she heard only the wind. "Yes, I said it! A cat! A cat who just runs off without a care for who might be worried about him! Whatever happened to loyalty? You know, that thing 'man's supposed best friend' is supposed to have?"

She heard nothing but bugs that were too far away to care where the ghastly noise might be coming from. She looked up at the orange sky. *I always wake up at dusk.* She chuckled. *Ghosts awakening right* before nightfall. There's probably something to that...

She yawned and stretched her arms up into the sky, toward the arms of the mighty oak at the center of the Harvey's property that reached toward the stars. Claire froze mid-stretch. The stars? I shouldn't be able to see the stars through the tree! The leaves that had been above her when she lay down were nearly gone. It was Autumn again. Or is it "Fall"? I wonder what the difference is? I wonder how many years I was asleep this time?

She turned and looked at her house. Her favorite tree lay too far off to hear anyone shout over the Midwestern wind that blew across the meadows, but it was close enough to see the kitchen and parlor lights were lit, plus a light from a room on the second floor. The sitting room above the kitchen. Claire sighed.

No. I must stay away.

She turned back to the meadow. "Rex!" She waited, listened, but didn't hear the familiar jingle she hoped to hear. What else could she do? She looked up and began counting the few stars that were only now peeking out from the fading daylight. But it was no use; she couldn't get it out of her mind. She had to know what was going on in that house. If anyone she loved still lived there.

Claire hopped up and stomped through the tall grass. She stopped when she reached the manicured yard. How long had it been? Weeks? Months? Years? She'd done as Max had asked. She'd left Sophie and Max's mother alone. She had explored the property. She had played with Rex. At least until he had grown tired of her, and blinked off into the great unknown, only to return when he felt good and ready. The first time he did so, he had stayed gone for days. The next time, weeks, then finally months. She finally got bored and took a nap, and of course, lost track of time, as she always did in the Meadow of Dreams. Rex could be anywhere by now. He could have found his way to Doggie Heaven! I hope you did, little Rex. At least one of us got out.

The nearby crickets and cicadas decided the danger had passed, and began to speak with one another again. Claire stared at the house. She didn't want to enter, but something gnawed at her. What if it had been more than six years this time? What if it had been twenty? Or fifty! If it has been too long, Max may be...

Claire pushed the morbid idea from her mind and ran up to the screened-in porch behind the house. It looked the same as she remembered. That was a good sign. But before she waltzed in, she remembered what Max had asked, and halted at the back door. She couldn't allow herself to be seen.

Claire concentrated, like she always did around Max's mother. As long as she didn't let her guard down or experience any drastic emotion while doing so, she could remain invisible. She had made a promise, and if Max was still alive, she didn't want to disappoint him. If he had passed on, she definitely didn't want to disappoint him!

She closed her eyes, focused on her core, and felt the familiar sensation wash over her. Now that it was safe to enter, she passed through the door and into the mud room, adjacent to the grand stair. Voices filtered into the room. Or was it only one voice? Did it come from the kitchen or the parlor? She waited, but the voice didn't come again. She leaned around the doorjamb and peeked left and right. No one was in the short hall. She took a step out of the mud room and leaned far into the hall, looking toward the parlor. Alone, she tip-toed to the parlor door.

No one was in the dark, mahogany-wood-paneled room, and both doors leading to the living room were closed. A fog hung close to the ceiling, which Claire thought odd. She heard the voice again. It came from behind her, in the direction of the grand stair. Likely the kitchen. As she turned, she heard a cough.

Behind her.

Claire spun around but still saw no one in the room. Brows furrowed, head low, hands raised in preparation to transform into her demon self, she stepped purposefully forward. She glanced about, wide-eyed, searching for the source of the noise. At the center of the room, where Max's father's pool table used to be, she paused and listened.

The cough came again. Claire spun to face the fireplace that separated the parlor and the living room. Before her, seated in one of the puffy recliners facing the brick fireplace, was a moving section of air. She could only see parts of it; the chair blocked most of whatever it was. She tiptoed around the recliners, and the squirming shape transformed into the transparent silhouette of a man. A hand rose to its head.

>Cough cough<

It was violent, unhealthy. She had heard her cigar-smoking grandfather make that noise toward the end of his life, right before he died. She gasped. Surely this ghostly man isn't my grandfather!

Claire inched around the other, unoccupied chair, never taking her eyes off the apparition. She remembered seeing this phenomenon before, on the day her life was turned all topsy-turvy, the day she began her life as Ghost-Claire. It happened when Bobbie's father had opened his mind to believing in phantoms—having finally experienced proof first-hand—and she had begun to see Bobbie's father rather than simply hear him. This man in the chair, whoever he was, held some belief, at least. "Who are you?" she asked the man.

He didn't answer.

She watched him bring a hand to his face. When he pulled it away, smoke billowed away.

So the fog that hung close to the ceiling wasn't fog at all, but smoke from a cigarette. Claire tried to smell it, but could not. She heard the voice again, the one coming from the direction of the kitchen. She cocked her head and listened, but still couldn't make out any words. She turned back to the stranger in the chair. "I'll come back for you later," she said, and hurried toward the kitchen, eager for answers.

She paused at the door and put her ear up to it. The voice was muffled, but she could at least understand the words now.

"He refuses!" the voice said. "He won't listen to a word I say!"

That voice! Sophie?

"I'm telling you, Max," Sophie went on, "I've just about had it!"

Claire's eyes grew even more wide. Max? Max is here? She closed her eyes again and, making sure she was still invisible, stepped through the closed kitchen door.

Max wasn't there.

Sophie leaned against the countertop, legs and arms crossed, and stared at the floor. She wore a glowing piece of jewelry in her ear. And she looked... old. Like thirty or something. Her once jet black hair was now sporting the tiniest bit of gray. "You can try to talk to him, Max, but I guarantee he's not going back to the hospital."

Claire's shoulders slumped. That glowing thing in her ear must be a telephone of some kind, she decided.

"I know, but he wants to die here, in his home."

His home?

"I think you need to get back here, little bro. And I mean like tomorrow."

Claire gasped. Surely that ghostly man in the parlor can't be—

"This weekend, then."

But, in all these years, I've never been able to see him, or he me—

"Don't worry about renting a car, Max, I'll pick you up from the airport. If you need to go anywhere you can borrow my car." Sophie shifted and put her weight on her other foot. "One of us has to be here with Dad twenty-four-seven anyways."

Claire's hand shot to her mouth. So it is their father!

>Thump<

Claire ducked, and her gaze shot to the ceiling.

"Oh!" Sophie looked upward as well. "Those darn kids!" She let out a sigh. "No, they're up in the sitting room; they can't hurt anything in there."

So Sophie has children. I wonder if Max does?

"Yes, growing like two little weeds!"

Another thump came from above.

"Two rambunctious little weeds." Sophie moved to the kitchen table and sat down. "How's Timmy? Did he make the team again this year?"

Timmy?

"Aww, that's great, Max! He's been wanting to play first base since he could hold a bat!"

Max has a son. Claire hung her head. That means he's married. She didn't want to hear any more. She turned and moped toward the door.

"All As and only one B?" Sophie continued. "Quit braggin'. Man, I'd be ecstatic if Jennie and Ralphie brought home all Bs. When they bring home an A it's a dream come true! That's wonderful. Max, that kid is so smart. He must get it from you." A pause. "Well, all of us didn't have their own private tutor like you did."

At this, Claire paused.

"Oh, God no!" Sophie exclaimed. "I haven't seen her since... well, not since Mom died. Before that even! Come to think of it, I don't think I saw her after you left for college."

Claire spun 'round. Their mother is dead?

"I kinda just assumed you had either taken her with you, or it was the dozen crosses I nailed to all the walls in my room!"

"I did as you asked, Max," Claire said under her breath.

"Or I thought maybe," Sophie continued, "because Mom was so sick, she felt bad for me and didn't want to terrorize me for once in my life." She took a long drink of iced water from a glass sitting on the table, and couldn't seem to swallow it fast enough.

"Nice? I was nice! I never did a thing to her! I think she took a fancying to you merely because you're a boy."

Claire scrunched up her face. Oh you did plenty to me, Sophie!

"Yeah, okay. Which one of us is more likely to know women better than the other?" Sophie stood up and paced the kitchen floor, arms crossed, her gaze toying with her surroundings.

Why, you... Claire searched her memory, glancing from one countertop to another and back again. You were selfish! Mouthy! Disrespectful! Maybe not to me, but to your mother! And to Max! And you... Well, you... But try as she might, she couldn't come up with anything that would warrant the severe haunting she carried out regularly on Sophie. Yes, she had been selfish, but could Mother have been right? Is that how "typical teenagers" act? And now, she was a woman. A mother.

"She did what? Really? Why didn't you ever tell me that before?"

Uh oh.

Sophie's hands went up, one to her face, the other to her chest. "Oh my Lord, she didn't! Now that sounds like the Claire I knew! Oh, yes, the ghostly wind, it's terrible!"

Oh no.

"She did what with her mouth? Oh, Max, I would have peed all over myself!"

He still hates me.

"Well, whatever you said, she must have taken it to heart, because I never saw her again. Nope. I think she might be gone. It's been twenty years, after all."

Claire gasped. "Twenty years!" she said aloud.

Sophie's head jerked toward the kitchen door.

Claire's hands clasped over her mouth, and she held her breath.

Sophie regarded the end of the room where Claire stood. "No. No, I'm still here." She seemed to stare right at Claire. "I thought I heard... something."

Claire turned and darted into the foyer, halting just beyond the closed kitchen door.

Sophie's voice carried through. "I guess it was nothing. Well, I need to go check on Dad. So I'll see you this weekend? Alright. Text me and let me know when your flight's coming in, okay? Okay... Love you, little bro. Bye."

Max is coming? Claire felt her face flush. Max is coming home!

The kitchen door opened behind her, and Sophie passed through Claire before she could get out of the way. The woman visibly shivered, and almost fell forward as she stumbled and stopped. She drew in a quick breath that was almost a yelp and spun around, her eyes wild and searching the space in front of her.

Claire didn't move a muscle.

"No..." Sophie shook her head. "No! God, no! I jinxed myself talking about you!"

Claire didn't make a sound.

"That was you I just heard in the kitchen, wasn't it?"

She didn't even breathe.

"Claire." Sophie spat, barely above a whisper. The hatred in her voice could have peeled the wallpaper around them.

Claire took a step backward.

Sophie spoke through clenched teeth. "I swear to God, if you really are back... You just stay away from us, do you hear me?" She fumbled for something in the front of her blouse, and yanked out a silver cross. She held it out as far as the silver chain would allow, her index finger caressing its shiny surface. "Our father is dying! Have some respect!"

Claire's back hit the wall. She turned her head and saw the kitchen door inches to her right. But why couldn't she escape through the wall? She was a ghost, after all!

Sophie looked toward the parlor, then turned back to face Claire, her voice once again a whisper. "Max told me what you did to him. He told me that he ordered you to leave us alone. You told him you loved him. If you do, if you ever truly did, you'll honor his wishes. And if you don't, Claire..." She raised the cross to eye level and stared over it. "I swear to the Good Lord above I will end you!"

A tear rolled down Claire's cheek.

Sophie stared directly at Claire, as if she could actually see her standing there, pressing herself against the wallpapered drywall. Perhaps she could; Claire's concentration had been broken, her emotions ran wild. After an uncomfortable eternity, the woman tucked the little silver cross back into her blouse, turned, and marched into the parlor.

* * *

Claire sat in a flowery living room chair, her knees pulled up to her chin, when Sophie's car pulled into the driveway along the side of the house. She didn't look up in time to see if someone else was in the car with her. Her gaze returned to the foyer. The sunshine made an oval of bright yellow light slightly off-center on the floor of the foyer, streaming in from the large circular window above the front door of the house.

The door flew open, and Sophie bounded inside. "He's upstairs in his and Mom's old bedroom. I'll put on some coffee."

Claire heard someone step inside, but the front door blocked her view of the new arrival. The Fall wind carried two golden leaves into the house. She stood and leaned to her left, trying to see around the door.

The large, ancient door closed, and Max was there, suitcase in hand. His long trench coat and fedora made him look more like a hard-nosed detective than the boyish teen Claire remembered. He took a deep breath and looked around.

Claire stared at him, not even daring to breathe.

Max dropped his suitcase by the door and took off his hat.

His hair! she whispered in her mind, as if he might hear her thoughts somehow if she were to think too loudly. His hair is now more gray than it is brown!

He looked to the right, toward the formal dining room, then turned and looked into the living room. His gaze fell directly upon Claire. Or did it? His eyes didn't seem to focus, rather, he looked right through her. Then he looked toward the back of the house, and possibly up to the landing of the grand stair.

Is it just me, or did his shoulders slump? Was he hoping to see me? Had he hoped I might be waiting to greet him?

Max hung his hat and trench coat on the coat rack. Retrieving his suitcase, he headed toward the staircase.

Claire breathed again. She had done everything in her power so that the boy she had grown to love— who was now a man—would not see nor hear her. The moment wasn't right.

He took two stairs at a time, despite his age.

So if twenty years have passed since he left for college, he is about forty now. Why is he already gray? Has he lived a stressful life?

She followed him up to the master bedroom.

There, Max sat down on the edge of the four-post bed. "Hi, Dad."

"How ya doin', boy?"

Claire's breath stuck in her throat.

I can hear his voice! So he really is a believer now! Or at least a partial one.

Max nodded. "I'm good, I'm good."

She stepped into the room and stood at the foot of the bed. To her, Max appeared as plain as the sunshine streaming through the bedroom windows, but his father looked like glass.

Max seemed to be holding his hand. His transparent, ghostly hand. "Did you catch any of the World Series?"

His father coughed terribly before answering. "Yeah, I watched it. I couldn't believe it. I never thought I'd live long enough to see the Cubbies win!"

"Yeah, that was something, alright!"

A pain stabbed Claire's heart, and she backed away. For the first time in his life, Claire realized, Max didn't know she was there. This is an invasion of their privacy. She turned and flew to her old bedroom. She would deal with the return of Max another day.

* * *

It was a "bummer" of a Christmas season, if Claire were to use Sophie-slang. Some friend of Sophie's named Billy had helped Max haul a nine-foot tree into the living room. Billy the Pig. He had eyed Sophie like a wolf would its prey one too many times for Claire's comfort. She was about to pull her old demon tricks on him and scare him off once and for all, but soon Billy left without a fuss, and Claire never saw him again.

She surprised herself taking up for Sophie, this girl-turned-woman nearly before her eyes, whom she still didn't care for all that much. But in this case, it was a matter of girls standing up for one another. And surely Max's once-spiteful sister wasn't that same selfish teenager Claire remembered? Claire admitted she owed this older Sophie a chance. Albeit grudgingly.

Sophie had done a beautiful job decorating the tree. Max helped, but his sister ran the show. Claire thought the silver ornaments and all white lights was a classy touch, much better than the multi-colored monstrosities the Butler family had insisted upon when Max and Sophie were children. Sophie climbed a stepladder to reach the top and placed the multi-pointed star on its perch.

Claire stared at it, and her mind drifted. She had spent a lot of years lying in the yard, on the roof, in the meadow behind the house, staring up at the sky. Dreaming of her Max. Of the memories with him that made this eternity bearable.

* * *

Before Claire knew it, Christmas morning arrived. Max helped his father down the grand staircase, or at least the outline of him.

Not being able to see the man disturbed her. To Claire, he was the ghost, not her. But she dared consider the fact she would have to endure it much longer. Their father—she remembered Max and Sophie's mother calling him Jonathan—was "in a bad way", as she had once heard someone say. She understood that to mean he probably didn't have long for this world.

Claire watched the meager gift exchange. It went quickly what with none of the children present. She thought it odd they hadn't come to see their grandfather on what could be his last Christmas.

Jonathan cleared his throat. "I do wish a certain grandson could have made the trip. I know it's a long way from New York, but I miss that little guy and that beautiful mother of his."

I guess I'm not the only one who thought it odd.

Max nodded. "They wish they could have come, too. Things just don't work out sometimes."

"And what was your excuse again?" Jonathan asked, his glass image motioning toward Sophie.

"Dad, you know Tom and I trade every other Christmas." Sophie collected two empty coffee cups. "It's his year with the kids."

"It was his year last year!" Jonathan howled.

"It will be okay, Daddy. They'll come visit on Spring Break and you'll have a whole week with them instead of just a couple of days."

"Spring Break? They're not gonna wanna spend their Spring Break in Northern Missouri!"

"Why not? There's all kinds of things to do here for kids their age! In downtown Kansas City there's all those fun things at Union Station, there's the new Aquarium and LegoLand at Crown Center, there's Worlds of Fun, Oceans of Fun, there's—"

"I wanted to see my grandkids on my last Christmas!"

"Oh Dad," Max exclaimed, "don't talk like that!"

"You know it, I know it, best to quit dancing around the bush!"

"You old coot!" Sophie called over her shoulder on her way to the kitchen. "You're probably going to outlive us!"

"Bah! I wish the Grim Reaper would just hurry it up! What, did he lose directions to our house? Max, get on your phone or your i-whatsit! Send him a text or whatever you kids do these days. 1414 Hollow Street. Tell him Jonathan Butler's a waitin!"

"Oh, you crazy old man!" said Max, standing up from the couch. He handed his father a thin rectangle with a glossy white side and an even more glossy black side. "Read your new book. I think you'll like it."

"What's it about? More of your para-whatcha-ma-callit silliness?"

Max laughed. "No, Dad, nothing paranormal; I know you never believed in my line of work and study. Like I told you earlier, it's a sci-fi novel, but I think you'll like it because it has Hitler escaping the Allied forces at the end of World War II through a time portal that Nikola Tesla invented. Or something like that."

"Huh. Maybe I'll skim it."

"That'll be more than you've done with most of the books I've given you."

"You know I can't see anything smaller than an orange these days, and yet you expect me to read!"

"The pad will read it to you, Dad. Just turn on the— oh, nevermind." Max snatched the rectangle away from him. "Here, I'll set it up for you. You won't have to do a thing but listen and fall asleep."

"That sounds like an okay deal to me."

Claire enjoyed their banter. Their father coughed a little that morning, but no terrible bouts like Claire had heard him suffering on occasion.

At close to noon, Max, Sophie and Jonathan gathered in the formal dining room for dinner. Claire discovered Max continued to call the midday meal "lunch" and the evening meal "dinner," but to her they would always be "dinner" and "supper." She couldn't smell the plentiful, delicious-looking bounty spread across the dining room table. It was just as well; it would have only upset her since she could no longer eat.

Or could I?

She had never tried. She had never been hungry. But now she stared at a small stack of golden buns on an oval, china plate near one edge of the table. Each bun glistened with butter. Claire licked her lips.

She maneuvered around the long table, giving Max a wide berth. She didn't want him to feel a chill in the air. Jonathan sat at the head of the table opposite the closed door leading to the kitchen. Max and Sophie sat on either side, near their father. Claire tip-toed over to the buns, which lay steaming between Sophie and Jonathan.

The family discussed politics—apparently some controversial figure had just won an election or something—but Claire could have cared less and wasn't listening to the details. She was more concerned with how she would get one of those buns off that plate and to her mouth without causing the entire family to lose their minds.

Perhaps she could envelop it in her invisible hands, and it would simply disappear from their view? If no one was looking directly at it when it happened, Claire reasoned, they wouldn't even notice it missing. Then she could blink up to her old bedroom and enjoy it. Or would she? Would her taste buds still work?

The discussion became heated. She took advantage of the distraction, and made her move. She snatched at the bun on the outermost edge, but only succeeded in making it topple off the plate. Dang it! She hadn't even stopped to consider it might be just as heavy as everything else that didn't belong to her. Maybe if I—?

Her throat constricted when she noticed Sophie leering at the bun, her mouth frozen mid-chew, her eyes as big as saucers.

Oh my God, she saw that.

Claire looked at the others. Max and Jonathan still debated politics. She mused she could have done a jig on the table in full view and those two wouldn't have noticed her.

Sophie looked at Max, then at her father, then back at the bun.

Claire held her breath.

The woman sat down her fork without a sound, and with nigh a word, placed the wayward bun back on the pile with the others. She then retrieved her fork, and dug into her turkey and stuffing as if nothing had happened.

Only then did Claire dare breathe.

Sophie peered now and again out of the corner of her eye toward Claire, then looked back to her brother and father.

If looks could kill, I'd be dead twice over. Claire took the hint, and decided upsetting Max wasn't worth a bun, even one glistening with delicious, warm butter. Especially not one she probably couldn't enjoy in the first place. She stepped behind Sophie and whispered in her ear on her way out of the room. "Thank you."

Sophie gasped and dropped both her knife and fork, each of which made a loud clang on the china.

Max and Jonathan fell silent, looking over in her direction.

Claire darted into the kitchen. Behind her, she heard the three plainly through the door.

"Sophie, are you okay?" asked Max.

"Yes!" Sophie exclaimed. "Yes, I'm sorry, I just remembered something I need to do later."

"Must have been something important to shake you up like that!" Jonathan said, coughing at the end of his sentence.

"Sorry I... It's not that big a deal. Ben! He uh... The doctor gave him some medicine the other day. I think I forgot to pack it in his overnight bag when he went to his father's house."

"Medicine?" her father asked. "You didn't mention he was sick."

"Oh, merely his bronchitis acting up again. He'll be fine, long as he has his inhaler. I really should check on him, though."

A pause.

Claire stood in silence, her back to the dining room door.

Max's voice came again. "You're sure you're okay?"

She heard the legs of a chair scrape across the hardwood floor.

"My phone's in my purse in the foyer," said Sophie. Excuse me."

"Sure," said Max. "I hope he's okay."

"I'm probably just being a worried old mom!"

Her phone is in her purse? What? Why would you carry a big ol' thing like that in your purse? Claire blinked into the foyer. She heard Max and Jonathan start up their political conversation again as Sophie strode out of the dining room.

Sophie made her way across the wide entryway until she came to a narrow, glass table that stood along the wall under a mirror. She dug into her handbag that perched precariously near one edge of the table, and pulled out a black rectangle with pink edges. It lit up at her touch, displaying colorful images.

Wow. Is that some new kind of television? Or one of those computing machines Max used to play games on? It's so tiny!

Sophie tapped on it for a few seconds while Claire watched. Then the little rectangle went black again, and Sophie dropped it back in her purse. She whirled around to face Claire. "I know you're here," she whispered, without moving her jaw.

Claire backed up.

"I may not be able to see you but I still have four other senses, you know! I don't need a sixth one to detect the likes of you!"

The jig was up. Claire resigned, closed her eyes, and let the invisibility cloak flutter away into the ether.

Sophie's hand shot to her mouth, probably to keep from releasing a yelp. Or throwing up.

"Shhh," Claire whispered. "I won't hurt you."

The woman's eyes started to water.

Why is she still so terrified of me? Claire stepped to her left, so she could see herself in the mirror behind Sophie.

Oh. That's why.

Her skin had peeled away something terrible in the last twenty years, her nose seemed ready to fall off at any moment, and one of her eyes was missing completely. She shook her head. Why only Max could see her in her purest form vexed her beyond words. Everyone else saw nothing but a gruesome corpse in various stages of decay. And after a hundred and fifty years, give or take, Claire looked like death warmed over. Literally. "Sophie, I promise I won't hurt you or frighten you." She looked down at herself. "Well, not any more than I am right now, I mean."

"Please..." Max's sister said, tears now streaming down her face. "Please just leave us alone."

Claire nodded. "I will. I promise. I'm sorry about what happened at the dinner table. The food just looked so good. I only wanted a piece of bread."

Sophie's shoulders heaved and she stifled a cry. She sniffled and turned her head toward the open doorway to the dining room. Her brother and father were still going strong with whatever they were arguing about. She turned back to Claire. "Look, I'm sorry this happened to you," she whispered. "I'm sorry you're stuck here. I know this is your house, but it's our house, too."

"I know."

"Dad... Dad won't be with us much longer. When he's gone, we'll sell the house, and you can have it back."

Claire felt tears welling in her own eyes. She wondered if Sophie could see them. "Sophie I'm sorry I was mean to you. When you were young, I mean."

She didn't reply.

"It was wrong."

Sophie nodded. "Thank you."

Max and Jonathan had fallen silent. Judging by the sound of clinking silverware, they had gone back to eating again.

Claire inched closer to Sophie to continue their conversation. She moved slow and deliberate so as not to frighten her, but Sophie still drew back. "I'm going to give you the privacy you deserve. It's only right. I won't bother any of you again."

Sophie didn't move.

Does she believe me? "I promise," Claire whispered. "I only ask that I can say goodbye to Max. I'll do it later, after... You know, after—"

"I don't think that's a good idea," his sister interrupted.

Claire narrowed her eyes. "Does he really hate me that much?"

"What? Oh, about when you—" She cut herself off. "He told me. But no, you silly ghost, he doesn't hate you. Claire, that was a long time ago. You two were just a couple of kids. Well, actually, you're still just a kid. I mean, yes, you've been in this house for well over a hundred years, but you've merely existed all those years. You haven't actually lived it, have you?"

She didn't answer.

"Max turned thirty-eight this year. I'll be forty-one in a couple of months. But we've lived all those years. We've experienced the world. We've both been through so much. Lots of relationships. Well, for me anyway. Max, he did things right. Married the first girl he met at the university. She, um, she looks a lot like you. I mean, like he described how he saw you."

Claire turned away.

"I probably shouldn't have told you all that. The point is, Claire, it took him a long time to get over you. His wife wasn't you. He wanted her to be you, though, and it nearly cost him his marriage. He was so depressed for so many years. He lost weight. He fought with everybody. He was so difficult to get along with. Mom didn't understand it, but I did. He had lost his best friend. He had lost the one girl— weird as this is going to sound, but I'm going to admit it once and for all—the one and only girl he loved. The one who could truly make him happy."

Claire stared into space, unmoving.

"He loved you more than he loved anyone, you clueless little girl!"

She spun back around, her eyes searching the woman's face for any sign of deceit.

Sophie sighed. "He still does."

"Really?"

Max hollered from the dining room. "Sis? Everything okay?"

"Yes!" Sophie called. "I'll be back in a minute! Just... checking my phone!" She lowered her voice to a whisper once again. "Yes, really. And that's precisely why you can't come back into his life."

Claire scoffed. "What?"

"He's doing well now, Claire. He's happy. Or at least content. It took him ten years—no, more than that—but he worked through all the pain. I got my little brother back, and Timmy's mother got the husband she always deserved."

Her face twisted. "You keep dancing around it; what's her name?"

"Claire—"

"I want to know."

Sophie nodded. "Miranda. We call her Randi for short. She's the mother I aspire to be. She's a wonderful person. I'm thankful she came into his life."

Her vision became blurry. She blinked away the tears. "Is she good to him?"

"Oh, yes, absolutely, she's an angel. You would just love her. We all do."

Claire nodded and swallowed hard. "Good."

"She wanted to come and finally see the house we grew up in, and bring Timmy, but Max talked her out of it. I guess... I guess he thought he might see you again, and—" She fumbled for words. "He just didn't want things to be awkward. He hasn't seen you since—" Sophie cut herself off.

"Since I hurt him."

Sophie remained silent for a moment.

Claire paced the foyer.

"I do want to thank you for not showing yourself to him. I don't know why you chose to stay invisible for so long, but I'm glad you did. I'm sorry, Claire, but if you came back into his life now, his emotions would get all mixed up all over again, and it would tear him and Randi apart. I guarantee it."

Her shoulders slumped. "I don't want that."

"I know you don't, Claire. That's why it's best for him to think you're gone. He's doing fine now. He has almost completely gotten over the loss of his best friend. His tutor and confidant. His first love. Don't destroy everything he has worked so hard to overcome."

Claire nodded. "I understand. I won't. I promise." Sophie's shoulders dropped, and her whole body seemed to relax. "Thank you, Claire."

"Sophie?" Jonathan called. "We need a tie breaker in here! Or at least a third opinion!"

Max's sister closed her eyes. "Okay, Dad, I'll be right there!"

"It's best I go now," Claire whispered. "Bye, Sophie. I hope you forgive me."

Sophie blinked, replenishing the streams of water that now dripped from her chin. She sniffled, smiled, and nodded. "I do hope you find peace, someday, Claire. I'm not religious, but I hope you make it to your Heaven. Someplace beautiful anyway. Far away from here."

Claire smiled, though she was sure it must have looked to Sophie like a skeleton with one eye baring its teeth rather than the genuine gesture she intended. "Me too." This made them both laugh a little. "Thank you."

"Bye, Claire."

"Bye, Sophie."

Claire stared into the red eyes of Max's big sister a moment longer. Amazingly, they had connected after all these years, and now didn't have time or prudence to enjoy it. She wanted to hug Sophie, but doing so would only give the woman a chill rather than filling her with the warmness Claire wanted to convey. Claire smiled one last time, then turned and blinked herself away, deep into the field north of the house. The Meadow of Dreams. Where she would sleep and time would pass, and she would know nothing of it.

* * *

Claire lay in the tall grass, staring up at the stars on a clear night. She had awoken earlier in the afternoon, and had no idea what the date on the calendar might be. The Moon and stars never changed except with the seasons. Maybe after a few million years she might tell a slight difference, but she couldn't imagine being stuck on this property for even another century, let alone that long.

A few hours ago her curiosity had gotten the best of her, and she checked to see if the house was still there. It was. Perhaps a year had passed from the Christmas she enjoyed with Max, Sophie, and Jonathan.? Perhaps ten? She didn't care.

At least that's what she told herself.

She oriented her body north-south, with her head on the northern end. From this perspective, the moon hovered nearly straight up but slightly to the left. It was so close to full it might as well have been so. Almost touching its right side danced the red planet, Mars. Peering further to the west, just on the other side of the great "cloud" of the Milky Way, the king of the planets shone brightly. Mighty Jupiter had nothing on Venus, of course, but Venus sparkled near the western horizon this time of year, and she couldn't see it right now for the tall grass. No matter; as her father had taught her about all the lights in the Heavens, it would come around again tomorrow.

She looked for familiar constellations, but with the grass so narrowing her field of view, she only found Orion, also nearly straight up. She didn't need to find any others anyway; the Mighty Hunter Orion was her favorite. It was the first one she ever remembered seeing as a little girl. She thought it was a butterfly until her father had told her otherwise. He often set up his telescope in the back yard, and one moonless night, he had it pointed to the orange-colored star that was supposedly Orion's shoulder.

"That's Beetlejuice," he had said with pride.

"Bettlejuice!" She only remembered it because that was the funniest name she had ever heard for a star!

She also remembered his mighty laugh. "Don't worry," he said heartily, "it's only pronounced that way. It's actually really hard to spell!"

Her gaze drifted down to the three stars that made up Orion's belt, and wished she could blink away to any or all of those stars, if only to see what was there. If only to see if each one was really a whole 'nother sun like her father had promised, with planets happily zipping around them. To see if any alien people like her—maybe even alien ghosts—

might also be staring up at their night sky at the same time she was, and wondering if she existed.

Or if nothing else, just to get away from here.

But if her prior, painful experiences in "getting away from here" were any example, she was certain a trip across the vastness of space would kill her, and permanently. Not because she needed air to breathe—she now doubted she actually breathed the air around her at all, it merely seemed so—but because this terrible, cranky old house simply wouldn't let her get farther than a quarter mile away without yanking her back. Nevertheless, she closed her eyes, and tried as hard a she could to blink away.

It didn't work, of course. It never did.

She couldn't blink to the Moon or to Baltimore or even very far across the street into the cornfield, let alone to a star that was probably a million miles away. No, wait, it had to be farther than that! How far away did her father say the sun was again? It doesn't matter.

Something far away called to her.

What was that? Claire sat up on her elbows and listened. "Rex?" She waited. "Rex is that you, boy?" When she got no answer, she climbed to her feet and looked back toward the house. The light in the kitchen was on. Something gnawed at her gut.

There it is again.

Should she investigate? Should she re-enter the house? The calling came again. She closed her eyes and tried to locate it.

South.

She blinked, and appeared at the edge of the manicured yard. The calling still came from the south. She turned right and walked around to the western side of the house. She stopped there and focused on the feeling. Now the calling came from the east, again toward the house. "Of course." Claire focused, wisped herself invisible, imagined the grand stair, and blinked to the landing. Once there, she stood in silence.

It wasn't long before she heard noises upstairs. She padded to the top of the staircase. A light shone under the closed door to her parent's old bedroom. What was now Jonathan's bedroom. She stood in the hallway, and pushed her head through the door.

Max sat on the edge of the queen-sized bed. Sophie lay on the other side, her arm draped across the empty portion between her and her brother. Claire looked harder, and saw the outline of a man in the empty space, making a depression in the comforter.

Jonathan.

Age-wise, Sophie looked about the same as she had the last time Claire had seen her. She had tears in her eyes, and her face glistened in the lamp light. Claire couldn't see Max's face, but his hair appeared a bit more salt and peppery than she remembered.

This is invasion of their privacy. I shouldn't be here. Why had she come back in? Claire turned away and focused on the Meadow of Dreams, but a moment before she blinked away, the gnawing in her gut came again. Much stronger now. Claire opened her eyes, whirled back around, and gasped.

Jonathan was no longer a mere outline of a man. Max and Sohpie's father became more and more visible with every passing second. Claire knew what this meant, and her hand covered her mouth to hold in any sound. Oh my Lord...

Then, for the first time in Claire's afterlife, Jonathan Butler was as solid and real as everything around her. He looked so much different than he had in the photographs of the family that still hung on the walls of the hallway. His hair was white rather than the ravishing black like his and Sophie's both were in the pictures. But he had that same handsome, rugged jaw line. Those same deep, dark brown eyes that gave Sophie and Max their good looks. He was simply—what was it his wife had called him?—more "experienced" now.

He breathed deep, blinked, and sat up on his elbows. His eyes met Claire's. "Who are you?" His voice was gruff, but not like it had been on Christmas Day.

Claire's attention shot to Max and Sophie, but they didn't move at the sound of his voice. Why can't they hear him? She closed her eyes and meditated for a moment, focusing harder than she ever had in her life or her afterlife, praying that Max wouldn't hear her speak from the ethereal plane.

"Answer me, young lady!"

There. That'll have to do. She opened her eyes. "You can see me?"

"Well of course I can!" replied Jonathan. "Who are you?"

"You're not disgusted? Or terrified?"

"Why would I be scared of you?" he shouted. "You're just a skinny little girl! It's you who should be scared of me! Now I'll ask one more time. Who are ya, and what are you doing in my house?" He looked at her nightgown. "And why are you dressed for bed? Did you just get up?" He turned toward the windows, which were all black. "What time is it anyway?" He pointed at her gown. "Is that ketchup? You need to clean that off before you get it everywhere!"

She tried to stifle a giggle, but failed. "Ha, no, that's not ketchup!" She couldn't help but smile at this crazy but charming man. "I'm Claire."

"Claire!" he shouted. "I don't know any Claire!"

She took a few steps into the bedroom. "I was a friend of your son's." She looked at Sophie, still on the bed. "And a friend of your daughter's, too." She thought that a true statement now.

"Was?" Jonathan said. "You're not anymore?"

"Well, yes and no."

"Yes and no? It can't be both! Which is it?"

Claire stumbled over her words. How could she explain this?

"Aren't you a little young to be a friend of my children? Why haven't I ever seen you before?"

"Well," said Claire, "you were alive before."

Jonathan froze at these words. "What on Earth are you talking about? Where are Max and Sophie anyway? Do they know you're here?" Then Jonathan—a second Jonathan—rolled off the bed, right through Max.

Max pulled his arms toward himself, and rubbed his bare skin with his hands.

"Did it just get cold in here to you?" Max asked.

Sophie's brow furrowed, and she raised her head and looked around.

Claire held her breath. Uh oh.

"What are you looking at?" Jonathan demanded.

She looked back to him. "You can't see them?"

"See who?"

"Your children!"

He glanced at the bed, then turned back to Claire. "My children aren't here!"

"Yes, Mr. Butler. Yes they are."

Sophie shook her father's body. "Daddy?"

"Well I don't see them!" he said defiantly.

"Daddy?" Sophie yelled.

"Dad?" Max put his hand on his father's chest. He then touched a finger to Jonathan's neck.

Sophie hugged him tighter. "Daddy, please wake up!"

Max sat back and took a deep breath. "He's gone, Soaf."

"No!" Sophie buried her face in her father's chest, and wailed.

Oh God. Claire shifted from one foot to the other. I don't want to see this.

"Young lady, what's gotten into you?" yelled Jonathan. "What in the world are you staring at?"

"Why don't you turn around and see for yourself!?" Claire yelled back.

"Well I just did, and I don't see anything there that's not supposed to—" His voice cut off, and he stared at the bed. His jaw worked, but no sound came out.

"You see now?"

He pointed at his body. "Who... Who is that?"

"That's you, Mr. Butler."

He turned back to her, then to the bed again. He shook his head violently. "No. No, that can't be me. I'm here. I'm standing right here."

"Yes, you are," Claire said. "And you're also there."

"But... How can that be?"

Amid Sophie's cries, Max's shoulders shook.

"You've passed on." It was all Claire could do to not burst into tears herself. "Just like me."

Jonathan looked back to Claire, his jaw slack.

"But that... That's impossible."

"Is it?" Claire asked. "You're talking better. You haven't coughed in the last ten seconds. You can see yourself lying in bed. And you can see me. You were too big of a disbeliever before to see me!"

Jonathan's swallowed audibly.

"What you can't see, Mr. Butler, are your children. They're on either side of your body there, crying their eyes out at losing you, even though you've been dying for years. I'm sure they knew it was coming, but losing a member of your family is still shocking." She added in a whisper, "Losing your entire family is worse, though."

"You can see them?" he asked.

"I've always been able to see them."

"Always?"

"Since the day they were born."

Jonathan looked all around, but moreso like he was searching his memory rather than for something physically in the room. "Oh my God." He turned to Claire, and looked down at her nightgown once more. "You're… you're the…"

Claire leaned in. "You can say it. Come on."

"You're the ghost girl! The one Max talked about when he was little. He said you helped him with his homework!"

She pulled on her gown and curtsied. "In the rotting flesh."

"And are you the same one who would haunt Sophie all the time? Just for fun?"

"Yeah, well, I apologized to her for that. We made up."

"You mean—" Jonathan stepped back and took a series of short breaths. "You mean you're real? You've been real this entire time?"

Claire nodded. "Believe me, I'd rather not be. I'd much rather move on to, well, wherever it is I'm eventually going to end up. But I'm stuck here. Hey, consider yourself lucky; you woke up immediately after you died. I didn't wake up for days, maybe weeks afterward. The entire house was cleared out, and my whole family was gone. It took me all day to figure out I was dead! I wasn't lucky enough to have someone around to break the news!"

Jonathan looked at the floor and shook his head. "I… I just never thought it would be like this."

"Yeah, me neither." Claire stared at Jonathan's body on the bed.

"Wait a second. Does this mean I'm stuck here in this house? Like you? With you? I remember Max told me his ghost friend couldn't leave the yard."

"Well, that's not entirely true. I can make it down to Old Man Moody's mailbox before the pain gets to be too much and I have to turn back."

"Who?"

"Oh, sorry. You never knew Mr. Moody, did you? I'm talking about the house down the road to the east."

"You mean the Taylor house?"

"Whatever," Claire said, stealing another line from Sophie. "Anyway, likewise, I can get about halfway to the Johansen's house to the west—"

"The Miller's."

"—and just over the creek behind the house. It's the same if I head south; I get about a quarter-mile into Moody's—er, the Taylors'—cornfield, and then I have to turn back."

"What did you mean by 'pain'?" Jonathan asked.

Claire took a deep breath. "It's about the only discomfort I've ever felt as a ghost." She rolled her eyes. "Discomfort! What am I saying? It's excruciating agony! I can't even describe it. It's as if—"

A bright white light shone from the windows and flooded the entire room, interrupting her. She raised her hand to block the light, which seemed nearly as bright as the sun itself.

Jonathan spun around to face the many windows of the master bedroom. "What is that?" he exclaimed.

"I don't know," Claire replied.

Jonathan moved to the French doors that opened to the balcony. He held up a hand before his face and peered through the glass. "Probably some dang kids driving around in the cornfield again." He made the motion of opening the French doors. They remained closed, but he moved through them regardless.

Claire followed him out onto the overhanging balcony, directly above the front door of the house.

"Hey!" Jonathan called. "Who's down there?" He leaned over the edge of the railing. "Get a move on! Or turn off your lights! One of the two!"

The light wasn't coming from the cornfield across the street, like Jonathan seemed to think. It was coming from everywhere. And nowhere. Claire squinted from the glare. "I don't think teenagers are doing this, Mr. Butler."

"Oh, now, something's generating that light! We just can't see—" He cut himself off. "Woah. Claire? What's happening?"

It took a few seconds for her to notice anything, but when she saw it, her jaw dropped. "Mr. Butler! Your hands!"

"Claire what's happening to me?"

She cupped both hands to her mouth as his extremities began to dissolve and flitter off toward the source of the light.

"Has this ever happened to you before?"

"Never! Oh my word! Your feet!"

"I'm... I'm tingly all over! I wonder if—" His chin rose. "Marion?"

Claire studied the space in front of him, but saw nothing but the intense, white glare.

He waved. "Marion!"

"Mr. Butler, do you see your wife?"

He nodded. "Yes! Don't you?"

Claire shook her head, but Jonathan wasn't looking in her direction.

"She's so beautiful. She's wearing that dress she wore on our first date. Marion!" he shouted. "I'm here!"

Claire smiled, and wiped away a tear. "Go to her, Mr. Butler."

"I'm coming, Marion!" Jonathan moved to the edge of the balcony and hit the railing. He looked down at his knees, which were disintegrating as well, but still intact enough to bump into things. As if that brought him back to Claire's reality, he reached out to her with what was left of his hand. "Come with me!"

Come with you? She looked back to Max, who was still sitting on the edge of the bed with Jonathan's body. Sophie lay next to him, heaving into the body of her father.

"Come on! Before it's too late!" His voice seemed distant, even though he still stood right in front of her.

She grabbed his hand. But her own went right through his.

No...

Jonathan rose into the air. "Grab hold of me!" he yelled from seemingly across a great expanse.

She lunged for his waist, which was mostly intact, and Jonathan reached for her. While she felt something, a resistance, her fingers couldn't find purchase. She fell flat on her face.

"I'm sorry, Claire! I'm so sorry!"

"It's okay!" She climbed to her knees. "Go to your Marion! Tell her I love her and miss her!"

"I will!" His voice seemed miles away now. He wasn't much more than a torso and a head, and even those were quickly fading. "Thank you, Claire, for all you did for my son! He loved you so!"

"I know!"

Jonathan smiled and then turned away, toward the light. Claire heard his voice one last time. "Hello, my Love..."

And then he was gone.

The bright light faded, the glow finally dissipating completely above the cornfield, and Claire was alone on the dark balcony. She scanned the star field to the south a few moments longer, hoping to catch one last glimpse of the "other side." But all had returned to normal. She took a deep breath, got to her feet, and walked back inside.

Max, Sophie, and the earthly remains of Jonathan all still lay on the bed. The two cried softly and held hands. Claire wiped a final tear from her face and tiptoed to the hallway as quietly as she could. The last thing she wanted to do was disturb them in this precious moment.

When she reached the door to the bedroom, she paused and looked over her shoulder. "Goodbye," she whispered. She smiled a tight-lipped smile, took one last look at the family she knew so well and loved so very much, and blinked out of their lives forever.

7

A New Family

"Haunted?" the realtor asked, her voice carrying from the parlor. "Oh no, don't be silly, Mrs. Newsom! I mean if you want to believe in such delly in this day and age you can, but I don't, that's for sure!"

Claire scoffed. That's a lie if I ever heard one.

Throughout the tour of the old house on Hollow Street, Claire had been able to see the realtor plain as day, which meant the woman believed in ghosts as much as Claire believed in dogs. She sat on the landing of the grand stair, watching and listening with little interest as the blonde in the gaudy purple dress finished her tour. The three intruders lollygagged into the foyer and stopped not far from her.

"It's Miss Sawyer," said the tiny brunette. With her short bob, she looked more Claire's own age than someone old enough to be shopping for houses with her husband.

The realtor blinked, her blonde beehive swaying. "I'm sorry, what was that?"

"We're not married," the male half of the couple explained.

Not married? But you're—

"Oh! I'm sorry," said the realtor. "I simply assumed—"

"It's okay," said Miss Sawyer with a big grin, "that will all change in a couple of weeks!"

The realtor's face lit up. "You're getting married! Congratulat-ee-o!"

"Thank you!" squealed the young woman. "I'm so excite-sees I can't stand it!"

"You don't believe the stories are true, do you?" asked the young man of the couple, who didn't look excited at all.

"Oh, of course not," replied the realtor. "These old, gothic houses from the Nineteenth Century have so much history, and so many people have lived in them, there are bound to be all kinds of cray-zee-zay-ney tales from that time period! Back when common, viggy folk were much less sophisticated and educated in the ways of science."

This lady and her slang! Claire rolled her eyes. And I thought Max and his sister spoke funny back in the late Twentieth Century!

The blonde stopped in the center of the foyer and turned to face the young couple. "Alright, if there are no more questions, everything looks fabu-lo-sees from what I can see. Mr. Newsom, if you'll press your thumb here, here and, um, let's see... here."

"Oki-dayo," he said in a perky tone.

"Oh and read over this last part carefully," the realtor said, and pointed to something on the transparent device she had just handed over. "Make sure everything in the purchase agreement is accurate."

Claire watched the man study the thing in his hand. Why this lady would print something as important as house-buying paperwork on a pane of glass was beyond Claire. All he has to do is drop it and poof! No more agreement! Idiots.

"This will go into the housing database immediately?" asked Mr. Newsom.

"As soon as I have your thumbprint on the final line," the realtor said. "Speaking of which, when you're happy with everything, your last print goes right here."

Well that's stupid. Don't they know you can just wipe thumb prints off a piece of glass? These people are bonkers.

"While you're going over that, I'm going upstairs to visit the ladies' room. That's really the only thing bad about this house: only a single bathroom! But, you gotta admit, it's one awesomely-dawsomly powder room!"

"Biggest one I've ever seen in a house of this era!" said the brunette.

"Okiday-way," Mr. Newsom called after her, his gaze fixated the little rectangle in his hand.

Claire still hadn't decided if she could live with this couple if they did indeed buy the house. They seemed nice, if a little batty. If they proved otherwise, she knew a few tricks. They would leave soon enough, just like all the others she didn't care to have around.

The lady in purple trotted up the staircase, which now creaked here and there with age. Claire followed her. Not that she was afraid the realtor would steal anything in a once-again completely empty house, she simply didn't care for visitors she didn't know.

Once the realtor reached the top of the stairs, she started talking out loud. "Charlie? It's me. I'm closing on the house now, so I should be home in an hour. Make sure you pick up Benji from school today— what?" A pause. "No! You know how I feel about that new nanny! She's complete moodisauce!" Another pause. "I know you just reset her memory but she needs her prime motivator flashed for sure, if not replaced altogether!" She stopped walking for a moment and stared straight ahead, pursing her lips and narrowing her eyes.

Claire walked around in front of her and studied her face, head, shoulders and sleeves. She must be talking on a telephone of some kind, but where is it?

"Charlie, you get the old one back! I mean it! I'll de-ex her! Oh yes, I will! I didn't have any trouble turning in the last one! If you don't—" She barreled forward, right through Claire. "Oh my!" The woman halted and shivered.

Claire shook all over and flicked her hands, as if flinging off a revolting liquid. "Eww, yuck!" she said aloud.

The woman spun around and looked from side to side, then focused on points further down the long hallway.

Claire stared her down.

"No, no, it's okay," said the realtor, "I thought I heard something. Whew! Brrr! I wigged a really bad draft just now! I should have worn hose today." She turned back around and made her way toward the bath. "Anyway, we'll talk about the nanny situation later. Just please pick up Benji today? Please-ies? Thank you, Charlie." There was another pause, after which her voice turned to a whisper. "Yes! Hold on, let me get into the bathroom!"

This piqued Claire's interest. When the bathroom door closed, Claire closed her eyes, and blinked herself inside.

"Okay, I can talk now." The lady in purple continued in a whisper. "Yes it was the last thing they asked. Well what do you think I said? I made it sound like it was all silly-billy-bay to ask such a thing!" The lady raised her skirt and dropped a set of frilly panties.

Claire had never seen the likes of them, nor wanted to. She turned her back.

As the woman did her business and continued to babble to herself, Claire moved over toward the double-sink and stared into the oversized mirror. She frowned. Oh my! What a rat's nest! She ran her fingers through her red mop in an attempt to untangle the mess. Ugh! I should have tried to steal a hairbrush years ago, when I had the chance! She shook her head back and forth, which always built body and fluffed her mane up like a lion. She bit the inside of her lip. That's not good enough. I can make it much bigger than that! She bent over and performed the fluffing ritual once more.

Behind her, the lady in purple continued. "Remember those stories the old man in the diner told me about the haunted places around town? Well I did some Googling. Get this. I told you about the teenage girl who was supposedly killed in this house, right?"

Claire stopped shaking her head and listened.

"Well, apparently it's true. And after her father found her dead on her bedroom floor, he took one of his hunting rifles and drove or rode or whatever down to the old Branton house and— Hmm?"

She held her breath, still bent over, not wanting to miss a word.

"Oh you know, the smaller, one-story ranch that backs up to this property. You remember, I drove you by it a while back. Any-hoos, so this Harvey fellow kicks open the door and, without a word, puffs out the boy's daddy-o. Cold blood. Right in front of the mum." The realtor finished up and flushed the toilet.

Claire realized then her mouth hung open like a fly trap, and shut it. Father? You did what?

"Well, yeah, klaa, of course they did," the realtor continued. "The judge reduced the sentence though. Called it a crime of passion after just losing his daughter and everything. But he still got Murder Two. Twenty years. Yeah they were lolly-lo lenient back then! But that was what, a hundred and sixty years ago? Give or take?" A pause. "Oh I don't know, the website didn't say. Disappeared into history."

Claire stood up straight, and closed her eyes. Oh, Daddy. Why?

"Her mother went on to marry a railroad tycoon. Used the whole tragedy to her advantage, sounds like. Totes votted a millionaire!"

Could it be true? Had her family fallen completely apart after her death? If so, it was little wonder she'd never seen hide nor hair of her parents! They'd never made it to Baltimore. At least her Father hadn't; he'd been locked up after avenging her death! Claire heard the lady turn on the faucet.

"Well no, a million dollars is nega-notts today, but back then it was like a trillion! Believe me, he was rich in his time."

And you, Mother! Claire wasn't surprised her mother hadn't waited for Father to be released from prison. She had run off with another man to try to forget. And one even richer in order to maintain her lavish lifestyle. But could I blame her? What would I have done?

"You know the Claire Marie clothing line?" continued the woman. "Yep! That's her! Named it after her dead little—"

The realtor's voice cut off abruptly. Claire opened her eyes. The woman was staring directly at her in the mirror.

Uh oh.

The bubbling blonde had distracted her with all the talk of her family. Claire had lost her concentration, her focus that allowed her to remain invisible. And since the lady was already screaming bloody murder at the top of her lungs, it was much too late to do anything about it now.

But honestly, have I really gotten that ugly that you have to scream so? I mean, most of my skin is still attached to my bones!

The lady whirled around to face Claire. She stopped squealing, and her eyes darted about, apparently searching for what she had just seen in the mirror. Then she spun back around, locked eyes with Claire's reflection once more, and started in again. Even louder this time.

"Oh come on!" Claire protested. "A lot of a hundred-and sixty-year-olds are missing their noses! And an eye or two."

The woman's arms flailed about, but her feet seemed glued to the floor.

Well, might as well have a little fun at this point... Claire took a deep breath, and levitated herself off the ground. She raised her arms, extended hooked, bony fingers, and bared every one of her not-pearly whites with as much ferocity as she could muster. Her hair and bloody nightgown billowed about in a wind that came from another plane. How the room always darkened when she did this, Claire had not a clue. But she thought it was really— and here she stole another word Max and his sister had liked to use so much—cool. She stared at herself in the mirror, concentrated, and tried to make her eye holes glow this time.

The realtor backed up to the sink, her face a twisted mess.

"Hey! Your beehive's blocking my view!" Claire shouted, but she was pretty sure it came out as nothing more than a banshee howl in the living world, considering the decomposed state of her vocal cords.

The woman melted to the floor, her screams degenerating to whoops and gasps. Lightning flashed around the room, surprising even Claire. Wow, didn't know I could do that!

The realtor scrambled to the door on all fours. Her fingers fumbled for the ancient doorknob, but her fingers didn't seem to work.

Claire floated up behind her.

The blonde stopped fumbling for the door, and she slowly peered over her shoulder.

Claire leaned close to her ear. "Boo."

One last "Aaaaaaahhh!" spewed from the realtor's throat right before the door flew open. The terrified woman fell in the middle of the hallway in her haste. She looked like one of Max's Saturday morning cartoon characters trying to take off, her arms and legs sprawling all about, her dainty heels longing to find enough friction on the hardwood floor with which to launch her body to safety.

Claire chuckled to herself. This is kinda fun. No wonder Sophie hated me back then!

The lady in purple all but tumbled down the stairs to the landing, still releasing little whoops and gasps as she tore down the smaller flight of stairs to the foyer.

Claire returned to her normal human self. The lightning, darkness, and wind died away. She wisped invisible and blinked to the landing.

"Sandy, are you okay?" Mr. Newsom asked.

The realtor hyperventilated her answer as the young man helped her steady herself. "I'm fine! I'm fine! Just fine! Um, my house! My husband rang. Yes! My stove was left on! My kitchen's on fire!"

"What?"

"On fire?" repeated Miss Sawyer.

"Yes!" shouted the realtor, dropping the rectangle of glass with the glowing symbols in her haste. To Claire's surprise, it didn't break. "I have to go!" The brunette shook her head. "But how could such a thing even happen?"

"I don't know! My housebot! It's on the fritz-o again! I have to go!"

The man scooped up the glass device from the floor. "Sandy! Don't forget your Googlie!"

The realtor stopped in her tracks, spun on her toes, snatched the rectangle from Newsom's hand, and bolted out the front door. She didn't even bother to close it behind her.

Mr. Newsom called after her. "So you'll call if there's any issues, right?"

There was no reply.

"I hope her house doesn't burn down," said Miss Sawyer, looking after the woman as she fled.

"Oh, absos," replied Mr. Newsom. He then turned to his girlfriend. "Well," he said, opening his arms wide. It's all ours!"

The woman's lips parted, and the whitest teeth Claire had never dreamed of assaulted her vision. "Yaaay!" the tiny thing screamed, and threw her arms around her man. "We have a house! A car! Neither of them are new but they're newsies to us!

And soon we'll have a family!" She patted her tummy. "And two weeks from now, we'll be married! Everything's shaping up so wonderfullie-sies!"

Claire blinked. You're about to have a baby and you're not even married yet? Did all family values disappear around the mid-Twentieth Century and never return?

"Oh, Bry Bry," Miss Sawyer went on to say, "I can't wait to start my new life with you!"

"I can't wait to start my life with you, either, Dar Dar."

Dar Dar? Bry Bry? Absos? Newsies? The cart before the horse? What kind of crazy world did these two come from?

"Oh my gods!" exclaimed Miss Sawyer. "Tiffani! She's still out in the car!"

Did you just use the plural form of "God"? And who's Tiffani?

Mr. Newsom shook his head. "Oh it's okay, I left the A/C on. She's fine."

"Well, I'll get her anyway. I'm sure she's hungry. I want to show her the new house!" And with that, the brunette trotted out the door.

Okay wait, so you two already have a daughter? Claire narrowed her eyes at Mr. Newsom. And you left her out in the car in the dead of summer?

Bry Bry, the boyfriend, cocked his head. "Is that a faucet running?" he muttered to himself, and headed up the stairs.

Claire stood her ground on the landing of the grand staircase, and allowed him to pass through her on his way to the bathroom. The man shivered, and she relished in his warmth.

"Whew! This old place is drafty!" He then bounded up the stairs three at a time.

She looked after him and scoffed. *I can take the stairs faster than that!*

"Here we are!" said Miss Sawyer from the front door. "Isn't it wonderful and quaint, and just all complete awe-snelli-ness?"

A low growl caught Claire's attention, and she leaned around the staircase to get a better look.

The young woman held a small poodle. Her brow knitted. "What is it, girl?"

The dog growled louder and seemed to stare directly at Claire.

"Tiffani, stop that!"

Oh. Tiffani is a dog.

The poodle continued its guttural assault, its eyes never leaving Claire's.

Still, they left their dog in one of those funny-looking glass-domed wagons out in that heat?

"Bry, are you up there?"

"Yeah. Going to the bathroom," the boyfriend replied.

Miss Sawyer rubbed her nose on the dog's head. "Tiffani, are you growling at Bryan?"

Oh, it's Bryan! Well that's a much better name than "Bry Bry." Claire walked down the short flight of stairs toward the front door.

The dog barked once.

"Tiffani! What's gotten into you? It's just Bry Bry up there, you'll see!"

Claire reached the half-way point in the foyer. This caused Tiffani to start rapid-fire barking. The racket was much louder than Claire would have thought possible from such a small critter.

"Bryan, come down! Tiffani's scared because she can't see you!"

Oh, brother. Is this girl dumb as a rock or what? Claire heard the toilet flush upstairs. Bryan would be on his way soon. "Hi Tiffani," she said as sweetly as she could.

The poodle stopped barking when she spoke, and its ears went up.

"I won't hurt you."

The growling was replaced with a slight whimpering.

"Shhh, it's okay, girl," said the woman. "Daddy's coming back here in a second. It will be okay."

The spry young fellow bounded down the creaky stairs, running right through Claire once again, and shivered like last time. "Brrr! Hey, girl!"

The animal's ears dropped and its whole body seemed to wag fiercely upon seeing him.

"See? It's only me," he said, patting its head with one hand and rubbing his now chilly arm with the other. "There you are, all better-sies now."

Tiffani licked his hand.

Claire leaned around Bryan so she could see the dog again. She hadn't seen a living pooch in a long time.

Tiffani's ears jumped up once again upon making eye contact with Claire, and the growling resumed.

The foreheads of Bryan and the young woman crinkled. They looked at each other, then back at the dog, then shifted their gaze toward the stairs. Toward Claire. No one moved.

Claire swallowed. Surely they can't see me? I made sure of that, but... Her gaze darted from side to side looking for any reflective surfaces she may have forgotten about. There were none.

"Bryan."

"Yeah, Daria?"

So it's not "Dar Dar", either.

"You don't think someone's up there, do you?"

The man froze. He seemed unable to move anything but his mouth. "Upstairs? I... I don't know..."

"Hello?" the woman called. "Is anyone upstairs?"

The poodle continued to growl and give Claire the evil eye.

"Go up there," Daria said, "check it out."

"I'm not going up there!" said Bryan, backing toward the front door.

"You were just up there!"

"That's before I thought someone might be hiding up there!"

Daria stomped her foot. "Well we can't just stand here all night wondering!"

"We can leave," he offered. "Let's go back to the apartment. It's getting late. Maybe they'll leave."

Claire scrunched up her nose. This man isn't acting like much of a... man.

"Maybe they'll leave?" Daria shouted. "Oh for goddess' sake!"

There are even goddesses now?

Daria tossed Tiffani into Bryan's arms and started up the stairs.

Well I guess we know who the man of the house is, Claire mused.

"Dar Dar!" Bryan called.

The girl stopped at the landing and looked back.

"Be careful."

Daria rolled her eyes.

Claire giggled. And you want to marry this coward? She relocated to the top of the stairs. She backed away when Daria reached her; she didn't want to frighten this girl away. Not yet, anyway. She was proving to be brave and strong. Claire was beginning to like her, despite her fears the brunette was as dumb as a tractor seat. Daria was probably only a couple of years older than Claire—or rather the age Claire had been when she died.

Daria switched on the hall light, even though there was plenty of daylight coming in through the open doors of all the second-floor rooms plus the bathroom. This was especially the case now that the windows in every room were once again devoid of curtains. She leaned into the master bedroom directly ahead. "Hello? If anyone's here, you might as well come out now. I'm not going to hurt you."

Claire's mouth fell open a little. She's not going to hurt them? Shouldn't she be more worried about a squatter or escaped prisoner hurting her? Good thing there isn't really anyone hiding! Is she daft?

"I'm Daria. Are you hungry?"

Now she wants to feed the likely dangerous, escaped serial killer? This girl was either the stupidest person Claire had ever met, or the absolute nicest human being in the world. Eh, I guess she could be both. Claire peeked into the master bedroom and saw Daria inspecting the walk-in closet, the master bath, and even the built-in cabinets of the seating area by the windows where Mother had used to curl up with a good book. Finding no one, Daria darted out of the room—barely missing Claire, who had to throw herself out of the woman's way—and tiptoed toward the eastern end of the hall. The hall branched into the sitting room to her left, and into the study to her right.

Claire blinked to the top of the staircase, in the middle of the long hall. Tiffani's soft growl floated up from the foot of the stairs.

Daria turned on the overhead light in the sitting room, inspecting the two shallow, narrow closets. She then peeked into the circular study, where there were no closets, and then resumed her tiptoeing back toward the stair. Even though Claire now hugged one wall, Daria shivered again as she passed by. "We've got to do something about the drafts in this house!"

"Righty-oh on that one!" said her boyfriend from the foyer. "So, nothing yet, Dar Dar?"

What a dumb question. Don't you think she would have told you?

"Nothing yet!" Daria answered. "Hello?" she called again.

Claire shook her head, admiration growing with each step this tiny but brave woman took, and each door she tore open. After "clearing" the closets of the guest bedroom and Claire's bedroom, Daria called to Bryan. "There's no one here!"

He let loose a heavy sigh from the first floor. "Oh thank the gods! Did you hear that, Tiffani? It was nothing. You were growling at nothing! Yes, you were!"

Claire gave her a side-ways glance. *You forgot a few places, you know.* She blinked up to the attic, glanced around, flew through the other third floor rooms, then returned to the hallway. *But don't bother, no one's up there.*

Daria shut off all the lights she had turned on and headed back down the staircase. "Thanks for the help, you big baby!"

"Well, I didn't know what to—"

"Come on, let's go back to the apartment and get some of our things."

"But wait a second, if there's no one upstairs, what was Tiffani growling at?"

Daria stopped midway down the stair. "I don't know. Maybe Sandy was wrong about this place?" She continued downward again.

"You mean about it being haunted? Oh, don't say things like that, Dar Dar. Especially now that we own it!"

Daria bounded down the last few steps and scooped Tiffani away from Bryan. "Oh, don't fretti-detti, my knight in shining synthetic. Maybe it's a friendly ghost?"

"Yeah," said Claire, blinking from the stair to the center of the foyer, "maybe I'm a friendly ghost."

"Well I don't want any ghost in my home, friendly or not!" said Bryan as he walked out the front door, shutting it behind him.

As Claire watched the young couple climb into their funny-looking, floating carriage from the sunny front porch, she pursed her lips. "Hey, join the club, buddy," she muttered. "I don't want a ghost in my home either. I simply don't have a choice."

* * *

A month passed without further incident. While the newcomers talked in an odd fashion, did silly things in their free time, and ate some of the strangest foods—Claire still didn't know what pepitas, "yog", and liquid aminos were—they weren't mean to each other or cruel to Tiffani. The little dog, in fact, was starting to come around. Tiffani now allowed Claire to at least be in the same room as her masters, if not near them.

Claire and the dog would both cock their heads sideways at Bryan and Daria as the young couple stared into space for hours on end, waving their arms and dancing all about, seeming to touch and grab things she couldn't see. Claire suspected Tiffani couldn't see them either. After a while, she got over her worry that they were psychotic or conjuring demons or something. It was as if they were talking on an invisible telephone or watching television, only she couldn't see or hear the moving pictures like they could. She suspected the small, transparent discs they slid onto their eyes first thing every morning was the secret. She cringed at the thought of touching her own eyeballs with her fingers. They made it look so easy! Claire shivered at the thought.

Occasionally Bryan and Daria spoke in a half-way normal fashion to themselves or others, and they laughed a lot. They celebrated Thanksgiving and Christmas. They ate breakfast and dinner and talked about their experiences at work, which often baffled Claire to no end. They could speak in gibberish for hours.

It might have helped if someone could tell her what a "Google" and a "Space X" were. Each word was written in colorful letters on lots of things around the house, even clothing. Bryan often talked about his "next quick jaunt into space", which Claire found very curious. She wondered how people could live in the space above Earth or on other worlds. Which they obviously could because the people in the white diving suits seemed perfectly fine when Claire saw them on the wall-sized television in the living room, walking around in the red desert they kept calling "Mars." Claire knew about Mars, just as she knew the names of all the other planets. And she absolutely did not believe people lived there, no matter what the television said.

When Bryan and Daria weren't talking in code or doing their strange dances, they cuddled on the couch and stared at their own little transparent rectangles that displayed lines of words like books did, or they watched moving pictures together. They made love, they fought, argued, laughed, cried, and entertained company on occasion, as a normal husband and wife would. They had jobs, even if they rarely left the house. Daria spent four days a week in the study, typing away at multiple screens full of gibberish. Bryan set up what looked like a fancy lab in Sophie's old bedroom, complete with computers and strange equipment, the purpose of which Claire couldn't even begin to guess. He also erected a small bowl-like thing in the back yard, and aimed it toward the southern sky. He called it a "satellite dish." Claire would often imagine he was trying to talk to people in outer space. Considering there were supposedly human beings living on Mars these days, she decided it wasn't that far-fetched, and wondered who might someday hear his calls. Father would have been absolutely fascinated by these people. By Bryan especially, even if he probably couldn't hunt to save his own life. He doesn't even own a single rifle! But these young idiots are okay, I suppose. I could have ended up with a lot worse!

Claire decided not to mess with "Bry Bry" and "Dar Dar" like she had with the realtor. She hadn't even meant to do that actually, it had just kind of happened and she ran with it. She smiled inwardly. She hadn't had that much fun since Sophie's snotty, teenage years. Sure, Claire now felt bad about tormenting Max's sister, especially after she had turned out to be a not-so-terrible person after all. But being, well, evil for lack of a better word—

It was fun...

8

The Neighbor

About six months after the Newsoms moved into the old house on Hollow Street, a new member of the family arrived. She came into this world in almost the exact same spot as where Max's father had passed on, if not in the same bed. Claire shook her head. I should have known there would be no hospital for people who call themselves "Vegans." Whatever that means.

Daria cradled the baby in her arms, blood and amniotic fluid still glistening on the newborn's tiny body. "Hi, Leselai."

"Leselai?" Claire spat. "What kind of crazy name is that? How do you even spell that? L-e-e-s... oh... lie?"

"She's perfect," said Bryan.

I don't know if I'd call her perfect. She might be cute once she's not so... disgusting.

It was when Daria and Bryan both wanted to take a bath with the little bundle of joy to clean her up that Claire couldn't stomach any more of their strange ways. She blinked herself out into the front yard, rather than the back this time. She just needed a walk. She looked left, then right. All directions but toward the east led to nothing but dirt, corn, grass, more grass, and more living people. At least someone she could talk to lived to the east. That is, if the thin man was still in Old Man Moody's house. Claire wasn't sure if she wanted to find out or not, but her feet took her that way anyway.

She slowed down when she got close to Old Man Moody's mailbox, and stopped when the pain reached the first hint of nausea. She took a few steps backward, and sat down. A car rolled silently toward her down the black road, which was now embedded with little white bumps every few feet, as far as the eye could see. Most of the fancy horseless carriages of this era floated between those white bumps, but this one had wheels. Claire had decided a while back that a car with wheels was better for two reasons. First, a wheeled car could go anywhere it wanted, whereas the floating cars could only go on roads with the little white bumps. Second, okay, sure, a "floatie" didn't need gas, but a car with wheels wouldn't come crashing to the ground if the electricity ever failed. She had learned of such things—along with scores of other technological wonders she could barely grasp—from the Newsom's wall-sized television. She, liked many of the living, could waste days staring at it.

A dog hung its head out the window of the wheeled car and growled viciously as it approached. Claire was in no mood. In a single heartbeat, the skin on her face flowered open, her eye teeth grew three inches, and she put enough energy to her empty eye holes this time to make the entire car illuminate in a green, unearthly light. The dog yelped and disappeared into the back seat as the machine rolled past. "That's what I thought," she spat, allowing her face to return to normal.

She looked at Old Man Moody's house. She couldn't remember the name of the new family that had moved in there. It was hard to keep track of the turnover of neighbors. It didn't help that she occasionally took "naps" in the meadow and didn't wake up for years. A pastel blue hovercar was parked outside the Moody residence. Claire liked the color. The house itself was now a boring beige. She wished it were white again.

From a window on the second floor, the thin, pale man stared at her.

So he is still there. She waved.

A second later, the thin man appeared next to the mailbox. He raised his hand, returning the friendly gesture, then sat cross-legged on the ground and stared at her.

Claire stared back, and neither of them moved for a good long while. She finally broke the silence. "Why don't you ever speak?"

He remained silent.

"I don't even know your name."

He tilted his head.

"Can I ask you something? When did you die? It was obviously before I did. But I mean, was it only a few years earlier, or more like a hundred? I can't really tell from your clothing; it's so ratted and all. But it looks much older than..." She trailed off.

He didn't say a word.

She shook away the chill that ran up her back when he stared at her with those white, pupil-less eyes. "So, did you die in the Moody house?"

No answer.

"Did you die in another house on the same plot of land, and then move into Mr. Moody's house after it was built?"

Nothing.

Claire took a deep breath. The summer sun felt good on her bare arms, which looked completely normal to her when she looked down at herself. She closed her eyes and raised her face to bask in the warmth. A crow called from somewhere far away. The wind billowed nearby trees. I should really get outside more. Maybe even head back out into the meadow? She could always count on it to take her away for a while.

Claire looked back at the thin man, who still sat across the road, staring at her. She looked to her right, westward on Hollow Street. A large, new housing development was being built up on the small hill in the distance. More farmland claimed to sprawling suburbia. She shook her head in disgust. She then looked south. The rolling hills, mostly cow pasture and corn fields, looked as untouched today as they had in the late 1800s, which made her smile. It's so peaceful out here. But why am I so... so... annoyed at everything? The muscles around her lips tightened, and her gaze snapped back to the thin man. "Is there something wrong with you? I mean, besides the obvious?"

He looked away.

"Can you even speak?"

He glanced back up at her, but kept his mouth closed.

Claire shook her head. Either he was a couple loaves short of a full bread basket, or he was being a jerk. Standing up, she screamed at him. "Fine!"

The thin man stood as well.

"I didn't want to talk to anyone, anyway! Especially not with a creep like you!" She turned and headed back to the house, stomping as she went. After several steps, she looked over her shoulder.

The thin man still stood by the mailbox. He hung his head, and looked as if he had just lost his puppy.

Claire stopped and turned back. "Wait!"

But as soon as the word escaped her lips, the man turned his back to her, and blinked away.

Her shoulders slumped. "Way to win over the neighbors, Claire." She turned back toward the house, and trudged her way to her own mailbox, which stood across the street from the house itself. The Newsom couple had repainted it to match their home, even though a box for paper letters was merely for decorative purposes nowadays. Apparently, the real mail had succumbed to something called "e-mail" a few years back, or so she learned from a news man on television. She had never actually seen this new type of correspondence, so she wasn't sure exactly what it was, but she figured she probably wouldn't like it. Similar to how she didn't like most other things in this odd time period.

"That's it. I'm going to sleep again," she said out loud to no one. Claire made her way out to the tall grass, found her spot under her favorite tree, and laid down. "Maybe this time I'll wake up and have a new family again. One that's not eating tofu and yogurt and nuts, and actually knows what hamburger is!" Not that she could eat or even smell a hamburger steak now, but she remembered what one smelled like in life, and she still wanted to try to eat real food again someday. But not today. She could barely even call the stuff Bryan and Daria ate "food."

She pouted a while longer, then relaxed her wrinkled forehead. The new development on the hill sprang to mind, and her eyes widened. "Maybe they'll tear down this old house and I'll have a new home to haunt when I wake up?" This caused her to sit up and look at her home one last time, in case she never saw it again. "If this is the last time, goodbye, old house. You haven't exactly been good to me, but—" She paused. Something occurred to her that hadn't before. The house! What if it's the house that is keeping me from moving on like Max's father was able to? Not God or Satan or Mother Nature or the Universe itself, but the house? She now looked upon it with disdain. "I hope you do get torn down, then, you evil old house! If you really are the thing keeping me here... I hope you burn!"

With a jutted lower lip, she over-dramatically turned her back to the old house on Hollow Street, lay her head back down again, closed her eyes, and forced herself into a deep sleep.

9

The Ghost Hunters,
Part I

Claire awoke to darkness.

She gasped and tried to sit up, but it was like she was stuck in molasses. She tried turning her head to look around, but that proved nearly impossible. She caught a glimpse of a faint light in the corner of her eye, but she couldn't make out if it was natural or artificial. Gravity was affecting her; she was not floating or flying. The temperature was extremely low. And if felt cold to her, it must have been freezing to the living. She could breathe, but then it seemed she could always breathe no matter what, even if she stuck her head in the bathtub.

She grunted and shoved herself upward, and her head poked free. She saw light so bright it forced her eyes shut. It wasn't the pure, white glare she and Jonathan had encountered when he had been "called home." No, this was merely sunlight. She was certain of this, for she could feel its warmth on her skin. But it was brighter than she expected, and she had to wait a moment until her eyes adjusted to the light. When she finally blinked them open, she understood why the world was so white. The tall grass of the meadow was covered in a good two feet of snow!

She twisted her neck around, farther than would have been possible when she was alive, and looked toward the house.

The rotten old thing was still there.

Her shoulders slumped. "So much for a new home." She focused on her situation. How has this never happened before? How have I never been buried in snow, as often as I came out here to fall asleep for years on end? Hmm. Maybe it has happened, and more than once, and I simply never woke up in the middle of winter before?

She pushed and shoved, expending more energy than she realized she possessed. The task of freeing herself seemed at times so difficult, she wondered whether she should simply stay put and wait for the snow to melt around her. I could easily "fall asleep" again and wake up in the spring. But what if she slept through spring, summer, and fall, and woke up in the winter again? And decades rather than years later? That might appeal to her someday, but not today.

Her arms were free now, and she put every ounce of strength she had into them to lift herself out of the suffocating, frozen, crystalline sea. In life, it would have taken her only a second to jump up out of the snowflakes. But now, in death, it took her the better part of an hour to wiggle free, one leg at a time.

Finally free of her icy grave, but exhausted, Claire lay on the snow a while. Not in it, but on it, like she might lay on an iced-over lake. Her head fell to one side and she looked at the old house. "Well, might as well go and see who lives there now," she said, and dragged herself to her feet. She took a step, and naturally expected the snow to come up to her knees. But instead she found herself perched on top of it. She took another step. It was as if it the snow was packed hard as ice. She looked behind her. No footprints.

Her eyes fell on the house again. Questions popped like firecrackers in her mind. Does the Newsom family still live there? Perhaps yet another family has moved in? I wonder what year is it now? What weird new things has the future brought me this time?

She caught movement out of the corner of her eye. Two deer hopped across the meadow and into a grove of trees not far away. That sparked a memory. "Rex?" She waited. "Re-eeex!" she called louder. As she listened and looked around for the long-dead beagle, Claire noticed several newer homes had been built on the properties adjacent to hers. Lots of them. She spun 'round to see whether the Branton's house was still there. Through the naked, winter trees she could easily see it was not. Where it had stood, an entire neighborhood of homes now lay. To the east and west, Claire saw similar growth. "Huh."

She turned and headed toward her home, being careful not to slip. she wasn't sure whether falling would even hurt—a fall from the roof hadn't—but it seemed careless to throw caution to the wind, even in death. She veered off her direct course to the house and headed around the side in order to see if the cornfield was still there. It was—of course the field was leveled and in its dormant phase—but it was nowhere near as extensive at it had been the last time she saw it. Houses had sprouted up toward the back of the field, probably about a half-mile away, too far for Claire to reach. Cars set in driveways or hovered down a street she couldn't see from her perspective.

She looked to the east. Old Man Moody's house was gone, replaced by a sprawling new sub-division. "Oh no." She thought of the thin man. Is he still on the property? Perhaps haunting a different house now? Or was he set free when the house was torn down? Should she try to find out? She tried to guess where Moody's mailbox had been, and pondered whether she could reach the first house on the corner of the new street without becoming too nauseated.

Questions entered her mind as she stared at the group of modern homes, which looked almost alien to her. Is it even worth it to try? Would I even be able to enter that corner house? If I stood outside on the street, would he eventually see me and come out to say hi? Would he even want to say hi, or does he hate me?

She sighed and turned to the west. She had noticed earlier that the Johansen's house was gone, too, replaced by more subdivisions. But now she could see directly down the street. It was a sea of houses that way, with no apparent end.

"Well," she said, turning to face the gothic structure beside her, "looks like you got lucky, didn't you?" She kicked a rock at the front porch. "You stupid old house!"

Preferring to sneak into the back rather than waltz in through the front door, Claire climbed the wooden steps to the screened-in back porch, which sported a new set of outdoor furniture. It didn't prove a new family had moved in; perhaps Bryan and Daria had simply made some upgrades? She stepped through the door to the mud room. Nothing looked different. Shoes and boots set along a wall, any of which could have been new or old. Nothing unusual.

A child's voice filtered into the room. "Momma! Orange, Momma!"

Well that's different.

But was it the baby girl Leelo-something? Now a toddler? Or had a new set of parents, perhaps more odd even than the Newsoms—

"You want some orange slices, sweetheart?" said a familiar, female voice.

Nope. Same old Newsoms. Terrific. I woke up about a hundred years too soon. Claire rounded the foot of the grand stair. Through a propped-open kitchen door, she saw Daria handing a plastic baggie filled with cut-up slices of fruit to a little blonde girl, maybe three years old. "Here you go, Leselai."

Eh, I suppose it could be worse. Mother used to say, "the devil you know..." Claire stood in the foyer at the foot of the stairs and looked toward the front door. The crown molding was still bright white, but the walls were a sickly green. "Yuck. Looks like the 1970s have made a comeback," she muttered, and let out a breath that blew stray strands of her long red hair out of her face. She turned to look back at the Newsoms in the kitchen, and noticed Leselai standing in the kitchen doorway. The little girl stared right at her.

Uh oh.

Leselai pulled a slice out of the bag and held it out to her.

Claire looked down at it, then looked at the mother. Daria was busy putting dishes into a machine under the counter top, a wonderfully magical device Claire had learned long ago was called a "dishwasher." She and her mother would have killed for one of those in the 1800s! She looked back at the little girl.

"Orange," said Leselai."

"That's right," said Daria, not looking up from her task.

The slice looked good. "I do love oranges," Claire said.

"Yum!" Leselai exclaimed.

"Yum, yum, eat 'em up!" said Daria, still busy with the dishes.

Claire bent over and put her hand under the small fruit. Leselai let go, and the slice fell through her hand and plopped on the floor. Claire sighed. Of course.

The little girl's gaze dropped as well. "Uh ohhhh!" she said, and bent down to retrieve it.

Daria looked up this time. "Did you drop one, honey?"

Leselai straightened up, and offered the same slice to Claire once again.

Her mother now had her head cocked to one side. "Leselai?"

The little girl turned to look at her mother, then back at Claire. Leselai took a step toward her, holding the orange slice higher.

"Sweetheart, what are you doing?"

Claire took a step back.

Leselai took another step forward, then looked down. "Ketchup!" she exclaimed, pointing one index finger at Claire's chest while the other fingers held fast the slice of fruit.

"Ketchup?" asked Daria, picking up a kitchen towel and heading toward the foyer.

Claire looked down at the blood stain on her nightgown, the one that always appeared wet even though it should have dried out decades ago. Never taking her eyes off the little girl, Claire reached out to her left and found the bulbous, wooden walnut that marked the beginning of the stair's dark brown railing. She side-stepped toward it, and her feet found the stairs. She started up, climbing backwards in a gingerly fashion.

"Ketchup, Momma!" Leselai said when her mother reached her.

"Why do you keep saying that?" Daria knelt down on one knee next to her daughter and pointed at the fruit in Leselai's hand. "No, honey. Orange."

Leselai popped the fruit into her mouth, yanked another slice from the bag, and put it up to her mother's lips. "Orange!"

Daria smiled and accepted the fruit with her teeth. "Yes, orange!" she tried to say, but it sounded more like, "Yesh, oranjzh."

Leselai turned back to the staircase and pointed upward. "Ketchup!"

The smile remained but Daria's brow furrowed. She stopped chewing. Her gaze meandered up the stairs.

Claire froze mid-step.

"Where do you see ketchup, honey?" Daria whispered in the girl's ear, not taking her eyes from the stairs.

"Girl!"

The smile faded in an instant. Daria rose to her full height and raised her head, her eyes now level with the landing at the top of the first small flight of stairs. She examined it as best she could from where she stood. "Do you see a girl right now, honey?" she asked, bending at the waist and lowering her face back down to Leselai's.

"Yeah! Girl, Momma!" she said, and smiled at her mother. Leselai looked proud of her accomplishment of correctly identifying various objects. Which apparently included dead people.

Daria looked up the stairs again and whispered. "Where is the girl, sweetheart?"

Leselai pointed directly at Claire. "Der!" she said, with the voice of an angel. "Girl!"

Claire backed up, expecting one more stair. Instead she stumbled backwards, releasing a yelp and falling through a waist-high, marble pillar that hadn't been there the last time she had been on the landing.

"Uh ohhhh," the little girl said.

Now lying flat on her back, Claire looked straight ahead and saw a pretty vase slightly wobbling atop the pillar. From somewhere below, she heard a gasp. She sprang to her feet and grabbed the vase to steady it, but it was as heavy as everything else she tried to move that she hadn't owned in life. It wobbled on its stand, and she didn't know if it was picking up momentum from the bump, or if she had made it worse when she tried to stop it. She gritted her teeth and squeezed the ceramic with all her might. But it was too much. The vase fell and shattered at her feet.

"Uh ohhhh," Leselai said again.

Claire stood there a moment, staring at the sharp pieces, afraid to move lest the shards cut her bare feet to pieces. She looked over her shoulder to her audience.

"Arf!"

Oh, great.

Both Daria and Leselai turned to see the family poodle come charging in from the living room, surely to see what all the commotion was about. The little dog jerked to a halt when its eyes locked on Claire's. It took up a cowering stance, and growled.

"Good to see you, too, Tiffani."

"Arf!"

Daria turned back to the stair, and visibly shivered.

"I need to work on my invisibility, don't I?" Claire asked Leselai and the dog.

"Arf, arf!"

Claire nodded. "Sometimes it doesn't work on tiny people and even tinier animals."

Daria swallowed before speaking. When she did, her voice was a rasping whisper. "Come on, sweetheart!" In a flash, the woman scooped up her daughter and headed for the front door. "Tiffani, come!"

The dog looked at Daria, then back at Claire. "Arf, arf!"

"Tiffani!" she screamed.

The little poodle ran after her.

Daria snatched her purse from a small table and ran out onto the front porch without so much as another word. While she waited for Tiffani to clear the door, she looked back at the stair where Claire still stood motionless over the broken vase. Then the front door slammed shut behind them, and not a minute later, Claire heard the now recognizable whine of a hovercar as it sailed off down Hollow Street.

She closed her eyes. Why, oh why didn't I just blink away at the first sign I was seen? But she knew the answer. She wanted to see what might happen with this new little one. Leselai did seem sweet, even if her name was "one for the books", as Claire's father had been known to say. Unfortunately a silly accident had gotten in the way of any possible new friendship. "Well," Claire said. "I guess that's that."

* * *

The hours and days passed. Claire lost track of how many. She lay on the toddler-sized bed in her old room and stared out the north-facing window. All the snow was gone, so she knew it had been at least a month, perhaps two.

She daydreamed. About Max. About Rex. About riding her horse in the summer sun. When memories of Stephen popped into her head—for they spent many a day riding together—she forced them away. If she lived her whole afterlife, she didn't need to think of her murderer ever again.

Her horse Velvet had just reached top speed in her dream when she heard a sound from downstairs. Claire's fantasy melted away, and she sat up.

Faint voices filtered up the stairs, but she couldn't hear what they were saying. She climbed off the bed, never disturbing even a single thread. It would have been a feat if she had.

"So, they finally had the guts to come back! I'll bet it's Daria. I doubt I'll never see Bryan again. That little mouse!" Claire reached the top of the grand stair and listened. None of the voices sounded like Daria's or Bryan's. In fact, she didn't recognize any of them at all. "Hmm. Must be the movers?" She shrugged and bounded down the stairs to the landing, where pieces of broken vase still lay undisturbed. It wasn't like she could clean them up easily; to her, each piece was as heavy as a brick. But she had discovered she could stomp on them all day long and they wouldn't cut her feet. So now, she stood among the sharp shards and gazed at the three men who had recently entered the foyer.

No… two men and one woman.

The woman looked incredibly tall and thin, and sported what looked like a boy's haircut in the back and a girl's hairstyle in the front. Claire guessed she had come straight from a funeral by the dark colors of her collared blouse and pants. I'll never get used to women wearing pants! Her short, brown leather jacket caught Claire's eye. It looked more for show than something a lady would wear to keep warm.

Of the men, one was bald with a bushy beard and black skin, and the other looked to Claire like a big 'ol country galoot who might seem right at home on a football field. They both looked to be in their forties or fifties, and wore fashionable clothing. Claire received a good impression of the group right off the bat; she fancied nice clothes more than the jeans and t-shirts Max and Sophie often wore in their time.

In the center of the foyer were three large, yellow crates with rounded corners. Each had the letters "G.I.D.E.O.N." stamped on its side in black stencil.

The front door of the house opened and two more men entered, also dressed fashionably. They carried yet another trunk, this one orange.

Oh, the colors in this century! And the living think I'm hideous!

The two new men sat the fourth trunk down next to the others. Both were young, probably in their twenties. One was Asian, the other looked like one of those Ivy League schoolboys Claire had hated in the movies she had watched with Max. The five of them now stood in a circle around the still-closed yellow and orange boxes.

So these are the movers? This motley crew doesn't look like any movers I've ever seen!

The woman held a little transparent, glass square in one hand, and waved it around as if she was dancing with it. "Raymond, where's Mr. Livingston now?" she asked, not taking her eyes from her dance partner. "Has he reached the continental U.S. yet?"

"His connecting flight was delayed, boss," said the galoot, smoothing his dark hair back after a long strand had fallen into his eye. "His last message said he was on approach to Kansas City. Said he figured he would make it here on-site around nine or so."

The lady checked her watch. "Hour and a half. Okay. Well, he won't be crucial until we can get a clear picture of what's going on here, anyway. Charlie, Horace, start getting the Gideons together."

The dark, bald man and the Ivy League schoolboy went into swift action.

"Raymond," the boss continued, going back to the small square she held, "I'm picking up vapors in the immediate vicinity. Looks like she's been here very recently. Might still be in the house. Get a net on this door and the back door immediately."

"Already got the emitters in place, boss!" the young Asian man said. "Just waiting for you to give me the word."

"Mikel, the word is given."

The one called Mikel tapped a button on his own small, glowing rectangle, and Claire heard a crackle. A green, glowing spider web appeared out of nowhere, completely covering the front door. Several glowing green lines appeared in every window, running horizontally. "Nets are on, boss," he reported. "As is the immediate perimeter fence around the home. The dome is going up also."

The woman they called "boss" raised her eyebrows. "Impressive. And I didn't even have to go over the containment plan again."

"He had a good teacher," said Raymond. "Good job, son."

Mikel grinned.

The boss' smile faded. "Yes. I suppose he did."

"How can you tell they're on?" Ivy League asked as he worked various latches on the boxes. "I don't see anything."

Raymond snorted. "Newbie. I guess you haven't got to the chapter on Apparitic Fencing?"

"Guess not."

"You should be way past that by now, Horace." Raymond gave him a stare that could kill a small dog.

Mikel leaned over to Horace and pointed to something on his device, then whispered, "We can't see it, but the ghost can."

So they're trying to trap me. Claire took a mental inventory as she looked around the room. Big galoot: Raymond. Asian: Mikel. Ivy League: Horace. Bald man: Charlie. Got it. I wonder what the lady's... name... is...? Claire lost her train of thought as her attention was drawn to the spider web. It had begun to undulate with intermittent pulses of light, creating hauntingly beautiful patterns. Her eyes glazed over.

"What about the window wells in the basement?" asked the woman. "Tell me we didn't forget those again."

"Not this time, boss," Raymond said. "Mikel and I set up mini nets on each one before we came in. They went up same time as the others."

"Awe-snelli-licious," the boss said. "Okay. Next we need to—"

Claire all-but tuned out their voices as she padded down the stairs. She couldn't take her eyes from the intricate ethereal webbing over the front door. She heard a distant beeping arise from somewhere, and a voice say, "Hold on. I think I've got something."

Claire walked directly toward the group of newcomers, mesmerized by the ever-more complex geometrical patterns of the webbing just beyond them. Movement directly in front of her made her blink rapidly, waking her from her trance, and she came to an abrupt halt. She found herself in the midst of the group, only a few feet from the boss, who was waving the glass and dancing around again. A silence had fallen, broken only by the wild beeping of the device the boss carried. Claire froze.

Everyone's gaze darted around the room. Everyone except the boss, who focused on the glass panel and walked around at the same time, bumping into the small table that used to be home to Daria's purse.

"You know, boss," said Raymond, "if you would wear the wireless lenses like everybody else, you wouldn't have to stare at your screen and try to maneuver around the furniture—"

"Shh!" the lady snapped, and turned toward Claire.

Claire stepped to the side and pressed her body against the eastern wall of the foyer.

The lady gasped and turned toward the men. "Do any of you feel that? That chill?" She smiled. "Boys, I think she's here in this room with us right now."

These people are different. They're actually looking for me, not trying to get away. I might not be able to... scare... Claire's attention was again pulled to the pretty spider web, but this time it only took a moment before she shook free of its spell.

They're trying to hypnotize me. Capture me!

She shook her head. Not today! Claire turned and dashed back up the stairs to the landing. There, she turned back to make sure she wasn't being followed.

The boss lady's eyes grew huge. "She is here! And she's on the move! It looks like she's operating close to a frequency of..." She tapped on the glass some more. "Damn! Lost the vector." She sighed. "But wow. Enough plas-metric energy's floating around here to light up the entire house! It looks as though she's been all over the place, not just cooped up in a favorite room like a lot of these little demons!"

"I don't know about you guys," said Mikel, looking all about him with eyes as wild as a feral cat, as if he could see through the walls themselves, "but I've never seen a house with this much plasmatic haze!"

Ivy League spoke up. "A lot of haze is bad, right?"

"The phased-plasma-UV has trouble seeing through it," replied Mikel.

"So how do we locate her in a fog?"

"If she's like most of the ghosts we've seen," said the boss, "once she figures out why we're here, she'll be doing everything she can to get away."

"Oh, I get it," replied Ivy League. "That means more activity, and a better chance to hone in on her frequency. But doesn't that also mean she has to be close by for us to locate her?"

"As a matter of fact, it does." The woman threw a glance at the galoot. "Sounds like your apprentice has been reading his manuals after all, Raymond. But I'm not worried; if this girl's dossier is even half-true, we won't have to wait long. I suspect we might have her frequency by the time Mr. Livingston arrives."

"Really?" said Horace. "That soon?"

The boss smiled.

"Oh yeah!" Raymond exclaimed. "Newbie, you might just get to see your first bust tonight!"

Claire's forehead wrinkled. "Bust?" she mouthed silently.

"From your mouth to God's ears," said the boss. "Did I mention I wasn't looking forward to being stuck in this one-horse town for our standard week?"

The galoot chuckled. "Only about a thousand times, boss."

One yellow box was now open. Two of the men, Horace and the bearded man whose name Claire didn't know yet, pulled a silvery, metal dome from it. They snapped small boxes onto its back, then long, pointy extensions to its underside. It was starting to look eerily like a giant spider. Painted right behind the head of the beast was the same word on the box: "G.I.D.E.O.N." Below it was more lettering. Claire strained to see what was written there, and whispered each word. Some words were huge and took her a while to pronounce and work out. "United States Department of Paranormal Affairs (U.S.D.P.A.). Ghost Intercepting and Demon Exorcising Optitronic Necromancer (G.I.D.E.O.N.). Her eyes nearly popped from her skull. "You're kidding me. There is really such a thing as a ghost buster? And it's built by the U.S. Government?"

"Goes together real quick, eh?" said the bald, bearded man.

"A lot faster than I thought, Charlie!" agreed Horace.

The spider was finished inside a minute. Claire watched Charlie touch a series of buttons on the metal arachnid's side, and it sprang to life. It rose up on all eight legs, and its jaw opened and closed repeatedly.

Please tell me that thing doesn't eat ghosts! Claire winced as she watched its two hind legs work a glowing, green length of thread from its abdomen, and spin it into a cocoon under its belly. Ohhhh no. Claire shook her head. No, no, no, no, no.

Just as fast as the cocoon was made, it vanished, and the machine lowered itself to the ground once again.

"Ready, boss," said the bald one called Charlie. "Now we just need Pete to get here and program it, once you have the frequency and whatnot."

Claire shook her head with more exaggeration and backed up to the wall of the landing. If she had a beating heart, it would surely be pounding right out of her chest.

"Oh wow, boss," said the lineman-sized Raymond, "look at this reading. My meter's really spiking!"

The woman nodded and looked up from her glass. "She's terrified. She's probably watching us right now."

The whole group stopped what they were doing and looked around, some faces betraying a little terror themselves.

The boss turned to her men and smiled. "As long as she doesn't know how to teleport yet, she's trapped. But even if she does—"

Claire didn't wait for the lady to finish her sentence. She closed her eyes and the world turned white, as it always did when she blinked away. The next thing she encountered should have been the tall grass under her favorite tree, but instead, something hard and painful slammed into her. She felt weightless for a second, then she thumped hard onto the surprisingly tall grass of the once-manicured lawn behind the house. She groaned and rolled over on her back. "What the—?" She opened her eyes to see a glowing, multicolored wall before her. "Where'd that come from?" she asked aloud, as a nausea arose within her. The wall went up and up, over the roof. She sat up on her elbows and looked left and right. It curved in on itself and disappeared behind both edges of the house. It looked just like—

A dome.

This is the thing that one fellow was talking about! And that wasn't all. Dozens of bright green threads wrapped around the house like glowing rubber bands. She suspected they were what she saw in the windows when Mikel turned on the spider web. The bands striped the house horizontally from the ground all the way up to the ornamental fence at the peak of the roof. Claire guessed the threads would stop her just as the dome had, or possibly grab her and hold her until someone could capture her. The spider webs were surely intended to do that! But if either were true, how had she gotten outside? She looked at the cellar's window wells. Each had its own mini-webbing. So did the small windows embedded in the roof, at least those she could see on the north side of the house. Surely the entire roof was wrapped in bands. Then how was I able to get out here at all?

The nausea was abating, but not fast enough. She groaned, closed her eyes, and allowed her head to fall back to the ground. Golly, what is this dome thing made of, anyway? Her brow furrowed when she opened her eyes again and looked straight up. Wait a second. What is that? A smudge had appeared in the sky since she had last enjoyed the stars, at least two or three years ago now, judging by Leselai's age. A little, glowing smudge. She didn't know everything there was to know about astronomy—her father surely still had much to teach her—but she was familiar enough with the heavens to know that little smudge wasn't supposed to be there. Could it be some new airplane? She gasped. Maybe it's a U.F.O! Like in those shows Max used to watch!

But as she peered closer, she noticed something else about the smudge. It has a tail... "It's a comet!" she shouted. I need to find out what year this is! Oh! I wonder if—?

The back door opened, interrupting her thought. The boss woman stepped onto the screened-in porch, followed by Mikel. "Yep, I was right!" she said. "She did make it out to the yard!" The lady held up her glass rectangle as she came through the screened door. "I told you, Mikel, you should never assume a ghost's abilities based on their age at death! Somehow she found a way out!"

"Good thing I turned the dome on when I did, and it had time to fully converge."

"Agreed, good job," replied the boss. "That's why we always double up with both fences and domes!"

"Yes, ma'am."

"This girl has had more than enough time to experiment and learn what she can and can't do with her demonic powers," said the woman, more to herself than to Mikel. "But I've never seen a ghost get through plasmatic-fences. I just don't get it."

Mikel looked back at the house.

Well, I guess they know I can blink away now. But what did she just say? Demonic powers? I'm no demon!

The pair grew closer, but each of them zigzagged about the yard in haphazard fashion. It was as if they couldn't pinpoint Claire's location or something.

Claire didn't move a muscle.

"Are you sure she's still here?" asked Mikel. "I'm only picking up what look like residuals."

"We would know if she teleported since we came outside." The boss punched at her glass.

"It will be nice when we get fielded version five-three-nine," said Mikel. "The new software will tell us precisely where a phased-plasma entity struck the dome's grid."

"We'd know exactly where she landed...?"

Mikel nodded.

"I'll talk to Callahan when we get back. The testing is taking too long. We need these new updates now!"

Claire sighed, and thanked God for small favors.

"With her activity so far," continued the boss, "I've narrowed down her frequency to within just over a hundred Hertz! And that was over the course of what, five minutes?"

"Not even." Mikel stopped several feet off to Claire's right.

"The range is a lot lower than most I've seen!"

"That makes sense," replied the Asian. "The energy this ghost seems able to command... it's almost like she's got the ability to hover on our plane full time, and not just haunt the place on occasion."

"You're right about the energy levels," the woman agreed, still waving her toy around a little ways off to Claire's left. "Off the charts."

So they can't pinpoint me yet, but they will if I stick around here and move around a lot. But if I can't simply walk through the dome, and I can't blink into the meadow—what did they call blinking? "Teleporting"?— how do I get out there?

The fact something like the dome stopped her meant she actually did travel between places when she pulled her little blinking trick, rather than simply disappearing in one place and popping back up in another, something Max had asked her about when he was little. If I can't go out, I'll have to go in, and try to hide until they go away. If I can remain calm, and don't move around, maybe they won't be able to see me in "the fog." If they can't see me, they can't capture me. Right?

But how was she to get back inside? Claire's eyes danced upon the house, from the cellar to the chimney.

The chimney!

It was nothing but bare brick and mortar, just like it always had been. No bands, no webs. "You guys forgot something," she sang to herself.

"Did you hear that?" asked Mikel, raising a finger to a small, glowing triangle in his ear.

Claire jumped up.

>Beep beep<
"She's here!" the boss exclaimed.

Claire concentrated as hard as she could, doing her utmost to wisp herself invisible, inaudible and untouchable to every living being in existence.

>Beep beep beep beep<
"Oh boy," Claire muttered. "Time to go."

"There it is again!" he exclaimed.

"Yes!" said the boss. "It sounded like someone said... 'Boy'... 'Time'... 'Go'..."

Claire's eyes nearly burst from her head. How are they doing that? She focused on the chimney, pictured the attic in her mind, and in the next instant, found herself standing on those dusty floor boards. She let out a deep breath and sat down in a corner. That was close!

An eerie, green light illuminated the room, thanks to the glowing bands that spanned the windows. She tried to sit still and remain calm, lest they use her movements and energy against her and capture her "frequency." Claire didn't know exactly what that meant, but she had recognized two important words on that spider downstairs: "Ghost" and "Exorcism." If there was even a chance that ungodly machine could send her somewhere, especially to Hell, she wanted none of that! She tried to come up with a plan of escape.

Absolutely nothing came to mind.

10

The Ghost Hunters, Part II

Denise Livingston-Bixby stood in the center of the parlor with her hands on her hips, and took in her surroundings. She noticed small discs scattered about the walls and ceiling that resembled tiny flood lights, and they triggered a memory of something Daria had said in her interview. "Raymond. What did Mrs. Newsom say her husband did to this room?"

Raymond looked up from his installation of a third panel in the center of the floor. Four more "slices of the pie" on a slightly raised platform would create a complete disc in all the colors of the rainbow. "What? Oh, he turned it into a holo-suite."

She grinned. "That's what I thought."

"Yeah, and those are Sony's new Zetta-Def series projectors," he said, motioning to the walls with his head. "As is Zettabyte Definition. With a roomful of those, you get vacations so real, you really do have to remind yourself you're still in your living room and not actually in the Caribbean."

"Nice." We can use this to our advantage. Her mind raced. If I could find a way to—

"Did I tell you I've got a holo-suite in my den?" Raymond interrupted.

Annnd, here we go. She looked down her nose at him. "I never asked."

"It's not this big and doesn't have half the bells and whistles as this place," Raymond said, apparently missing her tone entirely, "it's only Peta-Def, but it does the job." He lowered his voice and wet his lips. "You know, I'd love to show you around Florence sometime..."

Her tongue went into one cheek and her eyes fluttered. "You do know I'm not exactly single."

He gave her a sideways glance. "Denise, come on, we all know what's going on—"

"Just keep... setting up the Rainbow Bridge there, Raymond."

She turned back to the walls and shook her head. And just when she had been allowing herself to feel something other than disgust for her head tech... You're lucky you're the best field agent in the entire department, Mr. Parker!

"I see those gears a-turnin', boss," said Raymond. "And when I see that, I know you're scheming up something good."

"I'm thinking we can use this room to our advantage," Denise said, eager to return the conversation back to business. "Can you connect the Gideon's sensors wirelessly to this suite?"

Raymond sat there for a moment, slack jawed, his gaze flittering about the mahogany wood-paneled room. "Hey, that's a damn good idea! And with these high-end projectors, I'll only need to connect a few of them to get the full resolution of the Gideon's sensors!"

"How long?"

"If I only have to hook up five or six?" He mashed his lips together. "Probably an hour or so."

"And then if we can funnel the little demon girl into this room..."

"We'll all be able to see her with the naked eye! Hear her as well!"

She spun around to face him. "Bingo."

"No more aiming our individual phase-panels at her just to see mere wisps of where she's been!" He gave her a big, gross grin, and licked his lips. "Pretty slick, boss. Why didn't I think of that?"

"Why, indeed?" Denise turned her back to him before she threw up in her mouth. She looked upward, but focused on a point in space far beyond the ceiling. Attention all evil spirits, specters and ghosts: Your fellow demons may have told you... there's a new sheriff in town, and her name is Dr. Livingston-Bixby. Deaconess of the Church of Illuminous Saints! As per Father Benjamin's decree, empowered by the Hand of the Almighty God, each of you will be exorcised from this Earth! She gave the "Other Side" a wry grin and narrowed her eyes.

If not eradicated from this existence once and for all...

* * *

Claire sat in a corner in the attic, her knees drawn to her chest, and stared at the picture of herself and her parents. The sun had set. The only light was the green glow of the threads outside the windows. It was enough to allow her to find the loose board where her jewelry box was stashed. Not that she couldn't have found it by the moon and starlight. Or her "ethereal vision." But she didn't like to use that. Everything looked so... gross.

She caressed the fading photograph with her fingers. "I know I've told you a hundred times over the years," she whispered, "but in case this is the last time I get to do so, I just want to say I'm sorry, Father. I'm sorry I didn't listen to you. I'm sorry I ever gave time-of-day to that vile Stephen Branton. You were right about him. You were right all along. And I'm sorry you felt you had to take revenge on Stephen's father and ruin your own life. It was all my fault." She sniffled, and a tear ran down her cheek. "All mine."

She cupped a hand over her mouth, and her shoulders lurched. It took a few minutes, but she got a hold of herself. She took a deep breath to try to calm down. She had to, before she alerted the ghost hunters to her location.

"But in my defense, how was I to know he was going to kill me?" she whispered to herself. "I mean, who does a thing like that? Oh Father, if I could, I would take it all back. We would both live happy, normal lives, and you wouldn't have lost Mother to that railroad tycoon, and you wouldn't have lost me to that evil boy, and I wouldn't have lost either of you. Well, not until after a long, natural life, anyway. And I wouldn't be stuck in this attic right now, wondering for the first time in my afterlife if this is how I die. Again." She chuckled at the absurdity of what had just come out of her mouth. "Boy, did that ever sound silly."

She threw her head back against the wall and let out a long, slow breath. "Mother, Father, I've lived a long time. So long. Or un-lived a long time, whichever it is. If I die today—and I mean finally die, for good—it's perfectly alright. Maybe I'll see the two of you again? Maybe I'll see Max again? Maybe I'll just finally be able to rest? Like everybody else." She closed her eyes and tried to sleep. But in the same way she never ate or drank, she couldn't. She never could. The only place she could do anything that resembled sleep was out in the meadow behind the house.

Claire looked around the dark attic. Her eyes fell upon the panel to the sewing room. She shuddered to think what might be on the other side. There could be a web there. A ghost hunter. Or that giant spider waiting to exorcise her and send her to Hell. But what else was she going to do? Hide up here in the attic for yet another hundred and fifty years?

No.

She packed away her things, tucked the little jewelry box back into its hidey-hole, and forced the loose board back into place. She turned and faced the door. "Time to stop being a coward, Claire."

* * *

Denise stood in front of the parlor's fireplace, toying with a figurine she'd obtained from an illuminated glass display case sitting on the mantle. There were twenty or thirty in all, each from the late Twentieth Century, best she could tell. "Why people collect these silly old things is beyond me," she muttered, dropping it with a scoff. "What a waste of time."

"Are you kidding?" asked Raymond. "Those are vintage sci fi. That little guy you just tossed aside fetched a hundred and sixty-seven thousand at auction a couple of years ago."

She laughed. "You're pulling my leg."

"Not at all. Mikel is really into it and has several himself. That whole collection in front of you there would probably fetch a million by the right collector, easy. Even in only fair condition."

Her eyes scanned the group of figurines. "But they're all just so ugly!"

"Beauty is in the eye of the beholder," Raymond said, turning back to his work. "Everyone knows that."

Denise cocked her head and stared at the little masked fellow she had so recently disrespected. She placed him back on his black, plastic feet, raised his arm, and extended the pink sword-like thing he held in his hand. "Well, in that case, Mr. Newsom's an idiot for not having them in a more secure display."

"You find fault in everyone and every little thing, you know that?"

"Have you got the Gideon's sensors linked in to this suite yet?"

Raymond sighed, and didn't say another word.

Denise looked up at a large, round, transparent clock that hovered above the mantle. It was projected a few inches off the centuries-old brick. Its elegant, copper-colored hour and minute hands had been fashioned almost like skeleton keys. She admired its beauty, reminiscent of a simpler time. Before holo-suites and phasmatic-analysis and computers. Before Paranormal and Apparitic Science dissected the ethereal plane. Before ghosts became as understood as air and space travel for those in the U.S. Government with a high enough security clearance and a "need-to-know."

Her mind wandered. She thought about what it might have been like to live in this Midwestern Gothic house when it was new. Gone would be the sounds of modern life, beeping and chirping and ringing, abominations of electronic wizardry demanding her attention every few seconds of every single day of her life. "Mankind isn't supposed to live like this," she said under her breath. She closed her eyes and breathed through only her nostrils.

In... Out... In...

Her trance was broken when she heard footsteps behind her.

"Pete!" hollered Raymond, "s'bout time you showed your ugly face!"

"Ah, Mr. Livingston!" Denise piped up in her most cheerful tone, turning to face the newcomer with his scruffy hair, five o'clock shadow, leather jacket and tight-legged, European-style jeans. "Pleasant flight, I assume?"

"Oh, primo," Peter replied in a southpaw London accent. "First part of the trip was alright, but they lost me luggage at JFK. Then me flight to Kansas City was delayed three hours, and by the time I got there, the one and only car hire company left in all of America had no more cars on th' lot! I had to Uber all the way out here to the bloody Middle of Nowhere, U.S.A."

"Well, I'm glad to hear it was uneventful," Denise said, pulling out her plasmometer from her belt. She spoke fast; she had to in order to stay on top of the conversation, or Pete would do his thing and take all her power away. As usual. "Here's your update in a nutshell. I have the frequency narrowed down to within fifty Hertz. It's not ideal but I'm sure you can make it work, you always do. Horace and Franklin have the Gideons all ready to go, and number three is ready and waiting for you in the foyer. But I'm sure you noticed it already if you made it all the way here to the parlor."

"I did at that, Mum," he said, taking the plasmometer from her.

"Don't start with me."

"No problem, Guv."

"Pete, I swear, I'm not in the mood for your—"

"So you're using this room as Base HQ, then?"

"Turns out, this room is a holo-suite. So we're—"

He turned and headed out the door. "Setting a trap. Got it. I'll take a look-see at Bot 3."

Denise pressed her lips together and took a deep breath, readying herself to pounce.

"Blood pressure, Love! Don't forget what the doc said."

She let it out slow. In... Out...

"Makes your nostrils flare, too." he called from the short hall leading to the foyer. "Don't worry, I'll have the old girl programmed in a jiffy!"

Denise stared after him, and shook her head. "How does he always do that to me?" She shook it off and touched a spot right behind her left ear. "Mikel, status report."

"Far as I can tell the little gal's still tucked away in the attic," Mikel replied in her earpiece. "Hasn't moved since she popped up there about an hour and a half ago. Not that she could go anywhere now that the spiders have blanketed the chimney with webs, along with the pull-down stair."

"We won't be forgetting that again, will we, young Mr. Parker?"

"No, ma'am."

"Just so you know, Mikel—and so the rest of you listening in also know what's going on—your father is putting the final touches on the Gideon-to-suite link-up, and Pete arrived and should have Bot 3 ready within the hour. For now, sit tight and watch that hallway. If our little demon finds another way down, you're our early-warning system."

"Got it, boss." Mikel said.

Raymond piped up. "I take it she's still up in the attic?"

Denise turned toward him. "Did you turn your commlink off again?"

"The X-band transmissions interfere with this outdated T-31 Go-Synch module. Had Director Callahan approved the funds to buy the T-41, I might be able to—"

"Save it." Denise waved a hand. "To me you sound like Charlie Brown's teacher."

"Who?"

"Nevermind. Yes, she's still in the attic." Denise turned her back to him, put her hands back on her hips, and went through her mental list of the dozens of tasks her team had to remain on top of so they could get this job done tonight and head home tomorrow. She wasn't about to stay in this town longer than she had to; Amazon didn't even provide two-hour jet drone service this far out in the boonies. And she had promised herself she'd never 3-D print her Maine lobster ever again. Nothing beats the real thing. Things were falling into place, all except for one. There was still the problem of actually getting the ghost-girl into their trap. "What would make her want to come in here?" she muttered.

"What's that boss?" asked Raymond

"Just thinking out loud," Denise replied. "Trying to talk this out. What would make this girl want to come into this room?"

"This little lady seems smart. I don't think we'll get her into a trap very easily."

"Agreed."

"But we wouldn't need a trap if she hadn't fogged up the entire house with her crazy energy!"

Denise shook her head and paced before the fireplace. "These missions are ironically the most challenging. On the plus side, we don't have to wait very long to catch her frequency; high energy ghosts are easy to zero in on. But on the down side, high energy ghosts trail plasma all over the haunt site, and you have to be right on top of the little buggers to zero in on them. Ugh, listen to me, I'm talking like you."

Raymond chuckled.

"Chase a high-energy ghost around an entire house," Denise continued, "and all your precious electronics are worthless, and you'll be on the job for weeks. So you sit tight, and let the ghost come to you. Unless it won't come to you; unless it's somehow immune to the hypnotizing effects of our spider webs—and yes, fine, we've seen that in about fifteen percent of cases—but the trouble is, that makes the whole operation a Catch-22."

"Unless," Raymond added, "you have a holo-suite at your disposal."

"Right! This room is the key to ending this job quickly and getting back to the hotel and then back to New York! We just have to get her in here and the bots will do the rest. But how do we get her in here...?"

"Don't look at me," said Raymond, "I'm just the guy who makes the magic toys work."

"Yes, thank you, Raymond, you're an immense help," Denise said in a sour tone. She stopped pacing, and her gaze fell upon the tiny plasmatic-web emitters on either side of the wide fireplace. Her ever-calculating mind immediately formulated a deceptive course of action that made her smile. She snapped her fingers. "Got it! Raymond? Once Bot 3 is stationed in this room and actively scanning, I want you to disengage the net over this side of the fireplace. Leave the net on the living room side intact."

"You wanna do what, boss? Disengage the—? But the little bugger might escape if I shut it off!"

She took a deep breath. "Relax, there's still the net across the top of the chimney." Her voice turned dainty as she spun to face him. "But that right there is precisely the impression I want to convey. I'm counting on her believing she might have a way out. That will get her in this room, and from that point forward, the show is yours."

Raymond grinned from ear to ear. "Beautiful plan. See? That's why you're the boss, boss!"

"However, I don't want to make it hard on the bots. They might damage themselves in their eagerness if they climb up that flue. I want you to rig the web on this side to its own little button on both our screens, so we can flash it back on in a millisecond."

"Got it, boss."

Denise marched toward the short hall. "I'm heading out to check on Pete. Call me if you have any issues."

"Will do!"

Before she rounded the corner and entered the foyer, Denise stopped before a round mirror hanging on the wall. She roughed up the bangs of her fine, black bob, and gave herself a quick once-over to make sure everything was tucked away in all the right places. Once satisfied, she strode in with authority. Her stiletto-heeled boots clicked loudly on the hardwood floors as she sauntered up to Peter, who knelt on the floor while programming G.I.D.E.O.N. 3—or spider bot number three. His jacket lay next to him, his black t-shirt seemingly ready to rip itself to shreds should he flex a little too hard. She bent over and whispered in his ear. "Mr. Livingston?"

Pete grunted.

"After you're done sharing your calibration data with bots one and two, bring Bot 3 into the parlor. That will be its station for the rest of this operation."

"Not a problem."

"Oh and Raymond has a few configuration settings he will need to share with you. He'll fill you in on the particulars."

"Righty-o, old Mum."

"Peter, I'll ask you one last time. Stop with the annoying little names in front of the team."

"Denise, I'll ask you one last time. Get your suitcase outta me hotel room."

"Didn't you come straight here from the airport? Why would you think my suitcase is currently in your hotel room?"

"Because you stopped and primped in the hall mirror before coming to tell me something you could have told me over the commlink."

"Hmm." She breathed in his musky scent. "Looks like neither of us are going to get what we want, are we?"

He scoffed, and kept typing on the spider's small screen. "I still might. Me divorce lawyer's not done with you yet, Miss Bixby."

She grinned and picked a piece of lint from his tight shirt. "Did you know that in the olden days, it was the man who had to pay alimony to the woman? And usually lost half of everything he had in a nasty settlement?"

"Thank God th' dark ages are over and done with!"

"Oh, Petey, dear, do we really have to go through with this?" Denise asked with pouty lips. "You just got back to the States, we've been getting along so well all these months—"

"Over the phone," he interjected.

"—and everything just... fits into place when we're together."

He shook his head. "I let you fool me twice. That means 'shame on me'." He looked up and into her eyes. "No mo', madame batty. I'm only 'ere on a favor to Callahan. It's high time I blow this loony bin."

Her lower lip jutted out and she eyed him under low brows. "Oh, but that hurt." She smiled, and her voice became dainty once again, like someone flicked a light switch. "We'll talk later!" Denise turned up her nose and strode toward the front of the house. Not looking back, she added, "and it's Livingston-Bixby, by the way. Mrs., not Miss." She didn't listen for the scoff her little comment would surely draw.

She stopped a few paces shy of the front door. She first looked to her left, through the open air, double-doorway of the formal dining room. Horace sat next to Spider Bot 2, which had gone into sleep mode after not having a purpose for the last four hours. His spindly piano fingers punched repeatedly at his handheld device. She looked to her right, and saw Charlie doing the exact same thing, lounging next to Spider Bot 1. She then put her hands on her hips—her signature authoritarian stance—and cleared her throat.

Both men fumbled their devices—Horace dropping his—and hopped to their feet, facing her.

"Are we comfy?" she asked.

"Oh, yes, boss!" said Charlie. "I mean no, boss! But we're ready to go in the blink of an eye! You just say the word!"

Denise turned back to face Pete, who still sat at the other end of the foyer. "Mr. Livingston will say the word, when he's done programming Bot 3."

"Well," Pete called, loud enough for all to hear, "I'm gonna need a good hour or so, Mum. Fifty Hertz ain't nothin' to sneeze at, you know. Not havin' the exact frequency, I need to expand each parametric value on all twelve sensors to make sure we get a wide enough spread—"

"Wah, wuh wah wuuuuh, you've got fifteen minutes," Denise said, mimicking the famous

Peanuts teacher she mentioned earlier. She returned Peter's cold stare. It didn't last long; his blue-eyed steel gaze melted her. She did her best to not allow it to show outwardly. "Listen, I plan on getting re-acquainted with a bottle of wine and a forgiving husband I've not seen in ages by midnight."

"Sounds great," Peter agreed. "Just leave the bottle by me door."

She ignored that. "Hurry," she said with finality, and made sure her heels echoed across the entire house as she marched into the kitchen to rifle through her clients' cupboards for something that might take the edge off.

* * *

The maintenance panel between the attic and the sewing room didn't need to be unlatched from either side anymore. Claire could crawl right through it like she did every other door in the house. But before she did, she made sure she peeked to see what might be lurking on the other side. As fast as she could, she shoved her head through the wood and back again. The room had been dark, but had the same green glow as the attic thanks to the threads and webbing right outside its own windows. Huh. Whaddya know? She put her head back through the panel, and crawled through it at a snail's pace, lest these ghost hunters detect her with their magic devices. She thought it best not to teleport, because blinking seemed to generate more energy than anything else. She would crawl the rest of the way. To where, she hadn't quite worked out yet.

When her ethereal body was all the way through, she sat up and listened. She heard a deathly quiet. Claire crawled to the main door to the sewing room and peeked her head through with lightning speed, just as she had the maintenance panel. She knew this might expend more energy than she would like, but she also didn't want to give that mechanical spider more than a split-second to do whatever it might do to her. She had seen nothing; the hallway on the other side had been pitch black. Could it be hiding in the dark? Maybe it didn't emit any light when it was hunting? Maybe it didn't make any sound, either, completely shutting down to make itself invisible? Kinda like me? There was really no way to tell. If only I could have fit a lantern in my jewelry box...

Or a match!

She spun and headed back through the maintenance panel, then to the loose floorboard. In a flash, she plucked the small box of matches from her collection and tucked the jewelry box back into the wall. In seconds, she was back at the main door to the sewing room. But her matches were gone, her hand empty. Where'd they go?

She retraced her steps and found the matchbox on the floor of the attic, just on the other side of the maintenance panel. They didn't pass through with her. Oh, Claire!

It took a lot of effort to work the simple latch of the panel, but it came free in short order, now that she was used to this sort of thing. The panel itself was a bit more of a problem. She put all her weight into it, and after nearly a full minute, she had finally swung it open far enough to retrieve the tiny matchbox. She snatched it up and returned to the door leading to the narrow hallway, not bothering to expend the energy needed to close the panel. She pulled a single match from its box in the green light of the glowing bands. Before she struck the head of the match, she closed the box just as her father had taught her, so as not to burn the house down.

And then it hit her, and her heart sank. Claire, do you really think a match is going to go through this door when none of them went through the last one?

She dropped the box and the unlit match. Her only option was to open the big, heavy, sewing room door and peek out through the crack, hoping some of the eerie, green light might filter into the hallway. She didn't care to think how much effort that was going to take. She shook her head and dismissed the whole plan. With a sigh, she steeled herself for what might happen in the next few seconds, and barreled headfirst through the door and into the narrow hall.

Nothing happened.

Had the spider been there, it surely would have attacked, would it have not?

Claire waited with bated breath. Still nothing.

"Huh." Even though she couldn't see, she knew the hallway led to two other doors and a narrow staircase. The other doors were the third floor "extra" rooms, and the stair led down to the sitting room across from the study. If a person were in the sitting room, the small stair was hidden from view thanks to a door that resembled a narrow closet. It looked like a closet because that's what it had been originally. It was Claire's father who had commissioned a remodeling crew to transform the majority of the attic into usable space. Thus, the third floor rooms weren't in the original floor plans. The Newsom family didn't find the third floor for over a week, probably because, Claire guessed, their realtor hadn't known it was there. The jittery woman in purple probably assumed, like most every other visitor, that the attic was simply huge, dusty, probably filled with bats, and there was no reason to go up there. So this entire floor may have been overlooked by the ghost hunters, or just thought of as part of the attic!

Either that, or it was part of their trap...

For now, finding no one or nothing waiting for her gave her hope she would make it down to the second floor. But once there, then what? Fight? Sure, Claire, with what? Your macabre good looks? Transforming into her demon self was all she really had to scare away the living, but considering the profession of these newcomers, Claire figured that probably wouldn't work.

Escape. Get to the meadow. Go to sleep. Allow the Newsom family and the Paranormal People to forget me. But how do I get past the dome in order to do that? There had been a weakness in the ghost hunters' traps which allowed her to get to the safety of the attic, so there might also be a weakness in the dome. But she needed time to find it. And for that she would need a distraction. Expending energy was the only distraction she could think of. Of course, doing so would give her away, possibly allowing the ghost hunters to zero in on her. But she had to try. She could always blink back up to the attic if something went wrong.

Unless they decide to chase me up here next time...

Her mother would often say, "We'll burn that bridge when we come to it." With that advice in mind, Claire barreled into the darkness. She wanted nothing more at the moment than to give these hunters something to track.

* * *

>Beep<

Mikel stopped chewing his beef jerky and looked down at the "smart" plasmatic-device in his lap, which connected wirelessly with his contact lenses.

>Beep<

He tossed the wrapper aside and sat up from his slumped position in the hall, directly under the pull-down stair to the attic. He raised the transparent rectangle and touched a control. The words, "Phased-Plasma Panel" appeared at the top edge. He aimed it at the ceiling. It continuously fed data to his lenses and his earpiece, so he could both see and hear what his overly superstitious sister called "otherworldly" sights and sounds. She was right to be superstitious to some degree; ghosts were indeed real, if not every myth and legend she purported to be so. The living had just needed the right technology to prove it.

Enter the Japanese, Mikel thought proudly. Oh, he was proud to be American, too; were it not for the U.S. Air Force, which had been the catalyst for his father meeting his mother near Camp Zama, Tokyo, he wouldn't exist. But it was the Japanese, a world leader in electronics for nearly a hundred years, that ultimately found the key to making the U.S.D.P.A.'s technology work. Unfortunately, he could tell neither his sister nor anyone else without violating his Non-Disclosure Agreement—

>Beep beep<

Mikel hopped to his feet, turned in a slow circle, and waved the plasmometer over his head. Through his contacts, the meter would show him swirls of ethereal vapor should something existing on the ethereal plane move across its field of vision. But he had to be aiming it in the right direction at the right time for—

>Whoosh<

"Ah, here we go!" He aimed it at the trail that illuminated his screen like a comet in the night sky. Another whooshing sound entered his ear. "Woah. You're traipsing all over the place up there, aren't you, young lady?"

He tapped his earpiece once. "Dad? Dad, are you there? I'm picking up some really cool stuff up here!"

* * *

Claire ran from one end of the third floor to the other. She even blinked in and out of all three third floor rooms. Each had the familiar green glow of webbing across their windows, but none of them were inhabited by hunters or the spider. After a few minutes, she paused at the top of the small stairwell. "Hopefully that's enough."

She padded down the stair and paused at the door that looked like a closet from the other side. Once again, as quickly as she could, she poked her head through the door and back again. The sitting room was lit, but empty of people or machines. She burst into the room before realizing there could have been someone in the circular study across the hall. But luckily, it was empty as well. She let out the breath she had been holding.

And then she heard a voice. Her heart would have stopped beating, had it been beating in the first place.

"...thing I don't really understand," the voice was saying, "so it's a psychological thing?"

It sounded like Mikel.

"So she still thinks of the world in the same way she did when she was alive?"

They're talking about me. Claire took the opportunity of brief silence to peek around the corner. At the other end of the long hall, between her parents' old room and the bathroom, she saw the Asian man pacing the floor. He currently had his back to her, staring up at the door in the ceiling that hid the pull-down stair. His shirt glowed green from a spider web that covered the door above him.

So I guessed right, they did have me trapped. Or at least, they thought they did.

"Ah, right, Charlie, I get it," the young man continued. "Normally people can only go through doors and windows, so she still thinks in the same fashion. So you're thinking if she could go through the walls or floors, she would have done so already."

Claire's eyebrows lowered. *What is he saying? That I could walk through walls if I wanted to? Well of course I can! I'm a ghost! All ghosts can walk through walls, everyone knows that. I've done it a million times!*

Haven't I?

She could feel the wall behind her, touching her back, her head, her hands. She turned around and faced it. *Why couldn't I do this? Of course I can do this!* And with that, she bumped her forehead on the wall. "Oww," she said, and then cupped her hand to her mouth. She froze, waiting to see if she had been heard.

No sound came from the hall for several seconds, but then the Asian man spoke again. "No, nevermind, I guess it was nothing. Things that go bump in the night!" He laughed. "Unless there's a second ghost!" His voice dropped to a worried whisper. "There's not, is there...?"

Claire was vexed. *Why couldn't she do things every other ghost could do? Wait a second. The only other ghost I really know is the thin man down at Old Man Moody's. All the other ghosts I know about are just legends in the story books, or in movies or* on television! Huh. Maybe ghosts can't do all the things I think they can do?

As the conversation continued down the hall, her fingers felt along the striped wallpaper. The wall was as solid as every wall she'd ever known. But maybe that's the problem? I expect it to be solid. She touched the door to her immediate right, the one she had just come through only a minute ago. It felt solid as well, just like a door should. But she had moved through it as easily as she moved through air. She pushed her hand into the door, just to make sure she still could. Her arm disappeared exactly as she expected. Yep. Then why is this wall so hard to move through?

She stared at the wallpaper. What did that man say? It's psychological? She tried to push her hand through the wall again. No luck. She put her forehead against it, closed her eyes, and pushed. Still solid. Hmm. Maybe I need speed?

Claire stepped backwards, leaning to her left to keep an eye on the man in the hallway. She backed up until she bumped into the opposite wall. Okay, Claire, this could hurt. Or you could end up on the grand stair. Or even down on the first floor, where everyone is waiting to exorcise you! But she had to know if she could do this. If she could not, she had to learn. It would make fighting these trespassers so much easier if she wasn't bound by walls and floors and ceilings! She steeled her nerves, and launched herself toward her enemy.

She didn't bump her head on the wall this time. But she didn't pass through it either.

What in all the world?

Her eyes bulged when she realized what had just happened. She was halfway to the ceiling, on the wall. She didn't move. She had a death grip on the decorative, tulip-shaped lamp attached to the wall, afraid she would fall at any moment. She felt the force of gravity—or what she perceived as gravity, anyway—but it came from the wrong direction. It came from her current perspective of "down." She put pressure on her knees, as though she was about to stand up. Hmm. Is this more afterlife magic, or some kind of technology installed by the newcomers? Whatever it is, it feels like I'm on the ground!

She chanced letting go of the light fixture. Nothing bad happened. She tried crawling a few inches along the wall. Success! She rose to her knees. Again, she stayed put. Claire got brave then, and rose to her feet. She wobbled a bit, and dropped back to her knees. Okaaay, no standing on the walls. Not ready for that yet! But she could crawl along them. It wasn't as wonderful as being able to walk through them, but it was something else to add to her arsenal that she could use against the ghost hunters. She smiled. Time to sneak out of this house. She still had no idea how she was going to get past the dome and to her favorite tree in the meadow, but she would figure out something.

Clinging to the wall on her hands and knees, she crawled toward the hallway and peeked around the corner, which for her seemed more like "over" the edge.

"Each emitter has an eight hour battery life," the Asian man was saying, "but the matrix begins to collapse after about six hours, and is reduced in effectiveness by about ten percent every fifteen minutes." A pause. "Yeah, I hope we're out of here by then, too!"

Claire slinked around the corner and inched toward the grand stair, crawling on her belly along the wall as slowly as she possibly could, not unlike Max's childhood hero, Spiderman. She grinned.

Max would be so proud of me!

* * *

"Okay, let's see," Mikel continued, trying to concentrate on math while marveling at the ghostly images his contact lenses were providing him. "The emitters have been operating for about four hours now, so they're still at a good eighty-five to ninety percent of their full strength. I'd say you'd better tell Denise we need to switch them out with new ones in another two hours."

"Will do," replied Charlie in his earpiece.

"I'll pass it on myself, Mikel," said Raymond, breaking in to their conversation. "And I agree with all your numbers. Very good."

"Dad?"

"Sorry to eavesdrop, son, but I hopped back over to this channel to get a status report without the boss overhearing. Have you seen any more activity?"

"Not in the last ten minutes or so," Mikel said, spinning in a slow circle while gazing upward, making sure what he told his father was still true. "She seemed to have stopped moving. Just a lot of what looks like residual wisps swirling all over the place. And I mean all over the place. It's like she was in a panic or something."

"She probably is!" agreed Raymond. "By now she's figured out she's trapped up there and is probably going crazy!"

Mikel wasn't sure he liked the sound of that. "Um, Dad, you know how when animals feel trapped, they tend to be more dangerous? Do you think—?"

>Beep<

Mikel cut himself off mid-sentence and looked down at his plasmometer. "Hold on a second, my proximity alert just beeped at me again."

"What have you got?"

"Give me a second," he whispered, his eyes wide as he scanned above him.

>Beep<

"Okay, if the proximity gauge is picking her up, she's definitely within ten meters. But I'm not seeing anything specific."

"What do ya see?"

"Well, via the optics I'm not seeing anything I wasn't seeing a few minutes ago." Mikel shook his head. "Maybe she's inside one of the denser swirls and I just can't pinpoint her?"

"Sometimes, if they stop moving, they disappear from the scope. It all depends on their energy output."

>Beep<

"Which is why we didn't pick her up over the last hour or so, I know. But this doesn't make sense. When she was flying all over the place a few minutes ago, I could see what looked like the head of a comet, making trails all over the attic. I'm not seeing that now."

"Set the plasmometer's resolution to maximum setting, and use it like a telescope; the contacts don't have the resolution it does."

"But won't that reduce my range?"

"Slightly, but it won't be significant inside the house."

"Roger, switching over." He tapped a few virtual buttons. The contact lenses shut off and he was once again surrounded by darkness, except for the small, transparent screen he held. He adjusted the settings like his father had instructed, and then held the device at arm's length toward the ceiling.

>Beep Beep<

He held the device higher, and again turned in a slow circle, which, he figured, would cover every inch of the attic after one full 360-degree spin.

"Anything now?"

"No. I still can't locate her."

"Maybe she's above her old bedroom?" offered Raymond. "When frightened, ghosts often retreat to places where they felt comfortable in life."

Mikel moved into the room at the end of the hall, holding the device high above him. He shook his head, even though his father couldn't see him. "Just a few wisps; prior movement."

>Beep<

"Oh, I'm getting farther away, judging by the proximity sensor. It beeped twice a few seconds ago. I'm moving back to the hallway." He did so, still holding the device skyward.

>Beep beep<

He kept moving, walking past the bathroom.

>Beep beep beep<

He made it all the way to the top of the grand staircase.

>Beep beep beep beep<

"She's got to be right above me! But the meter isn't picking anything up! I just don't get it!" Mikel turned the device downward so he could view the hallway itself. At the other end, the lamps in what he understood was the "sitting room" provided faint light, and the lights from the foyer filtered partially up the stairs, but overall, the hall was dark. But at the edges of his plasmometer's screen, there was a soft, white glow. He narrowed his eyes. "Well, that's odd."

>Beep beep beep beep<

"What is it son?"

"My meter must be out of alignment. I'm going to readjust it." Standing at the top of the stair, he brought the hand-held meter down to his chest to more easily reconfigure the settings. As he did so, a white blur flashed across his vision, then the world went back to normal.

"What the hell?"

>Beep beep beep beep beep beep<

Mikel froze as realization dawned on him. He didn't blink, he didn't breathe. He carefully brought his "smart" device back up, slowly and deliberately. The higher it rose, the whiter the world became, tracking whatever it was his phased-plasma measuring device sensed, until he could see nothing but a fuzzy glare filling his entire field of view.

"Son! What is it? What do you see?"

>Beep beep beep beep beep<

He jerked the device up to eye level, and a black skull met his gaze against the blinding white background, and beside it, ten bony fingers dug into the wall mere inches away. He screamed and jerked backwards. The skull's jaw flew open farther than was natural, and the ghost returned his sentiment in an ear-piercing howl.

The plasmometer flew from his hand and he clutched his ears, lest blood spew forth and cover the wall on either side. His eyes clenched shut and watered, the sides of his head ached, and he released his terror in yelp after yelp as he backed away, still hearing the soul-stealing, siren squeal through his earpiece. He yanked it from his ear and mashed his hand against his head again, then tripped over his own two feet and came crashing hard on his tail bone to the hardwood floor.

He cried out in pain, and only then noticed silence had returned. Mikel's eyelids snapped open, revealing darkness. He ripped his hands from his head and yelled, "She's here! At the top of the stairs! She's right on top of me!"

* * *

Claire rolled her eyes and swore. I wish I had learned how to knock people out! She cocked her head at the young man. "Thanks, buddy," she said under her breath.

A voice filtered up from the first floor. "Mikel! Mikel!"

She heard footsteps on the staircase. Well, that's my cue! Claire pushed off from the edge where the hallway met the staircase wall, and leapt to the opposite wall.

Below her, Raymond took the stairs two at a time. He was surprisingly fast for such a big galoot.

"Hello again! Look what I can do now!" She said it more to herself than to him. She peeked around the corner to glance at Mikel, to make sure he wasn't hurt too badly. He had propped himself up in front of the bathroom door, gritting his teeth and rubbing his backside. "You'll be alright," she said aloud.

He gasped at the sound of her voice, and looked upward with eyes the size of dinner plates. Can he still see me even without his toy? Can he actually understand me, I wonder? Or do my words sound like nothing but a guttural growl to his ears? She smiled at him—or more likely bared her fangs—and hopped over to the wall above the landing. Below her, the boss woman was at the foot of the stairs shouting orders, a glass of red wine in her hand. A tink-tink-tink sound came from somewhere near the front door. Claire couldn't see the door from her high vantage point but she guessed what might make sounds like that.

The spider.

Should she risk teleporting now that she'd been seen? Had they already zeroed-in on her and acquired her "frequency"? She made sure she was invisible to normal human eyes, but probably not machine eyes. I wonder how fast it is? Probably not very. It's a machine with a bunch of metal legs, after all. How fast could it—?

The spider was nearly at the foot of the stairs already, and shot a glowing, green thread from its abdomen directly at Claire's head. She immediately blinked a foot to the left, but still felt the heat of the glowing string as it brushed past her ear. Okay, I was wrong, they can move pretty fast!

A second spider zipped along the wall that the foyer shared with the dining room and kitchen, defying gravity, spewing forth a stream of green that coiled and spread itself wide.

Woah, there are two of them!? Claire blinked over to the wall in front of her, high above the first step of the grand stair. The coil of thread thwacked hard where she had just been. It stayed put, like a wet spaghetti noodle thrown against a wall. Eww!

The first spider was now on the stairs, silently negotiating the carpeted steps with an agility Claire had never seen in a machine before. It paused, didn't bother to turn to face her, yet still shot a thread from its backside with all the accuracy of a sharpshooter.

Claire leapt to her right, into the corner. It doesn't even have to be looking at me to fire a web! Just then a new thread splattered right next to her. This one from a third spider.

Three!? She waited for the next attack, and wondered why it didn't come immediately. Did these things need a few seconds to recharge between shots? Maybe they—?

The second spider had sneaked underneath her on the ceiling below, and now peeked at her upside down, only inches away. "Ahh!" she yelped, and blinked away. She arrived in the middle of the kitchen floor a millisecond later. She yelped again as a searing pain shot through her forearm. She looked down to see round patches where her skin seemed to be melting. Had some of the green goo splattered onto her?

"Did everyone hear that?" The woman yelled from the open kitchen door.

"Where'd she go?" someone hollered from a distance.

"I don't know!" the boss hollered back, "my screen's completely white!" She spun, searching all around with her little see-through rectangle.

Claire touched her burned skin with tender fingertips, dark, open holes emerging on her left forearm. She clenched her teeth. Now I remember what pain feels like... She wondered if such an injury could ever heal in the spirit world. She closed her eyes, and a tear streamed down her cheek. "Why do you people hate me so?"

When she opened her eyes again, the woman with the midnight hair that ended in points at her collarbones stared right at Claire, holding her little rectangle out in front of her.

Claire dared not move, even though she was now sure she had been seen. Through the transparent device the lady held, Claire could plainly see the woman's face. An evil grin spread from ear to ear.

"I don't hate you," the woman replied. "I just want to send you home."

Claire let out a whimper, and felt as though she could melt through the floorboards at any moment. Right then, she wished she could.

"Don't you want to go home, little demoness?"

She backed up to the wall.

"I can send you there, Miss Harvey," the boss added.

Her breath caught. "How do you know my name?"

"I know a lot of things about you. Come. Follow me." She took a step backward.

Claire shook her head. "Never." But where else can I go?

The woman was all the way out of the kitchen now. "I'll take you home, Claire."

Out of the corner of her eye, Claire concentrated on the door to the cellar.

"Bot 2!" the boss yelled.

She heard the tink-tink-tink of the spiders' feet on the wall just outside the door. The moment Claire saw the spider enter the kitchen, she closed her eyes. When she opened them, she was at the bottom of the cellar's wooden stair, under the floor of the foyer. She allowed herself to breathe again.

To her surprise, her bare feet told her she was not standing on dirt, but something else. She suspected it was that stuff Max had called linoleum, because it felt exactly the same as the floor in the bathroom. She shook her head. Why are you worried about linoleum right now, you moron? There are three of those terrible tarantulas after you! She had to find somewhere to hide from these crafty ghost hunters and their lightning-fast nightmare machines. And quick. She would not underestimate any of them again.

"Mr. Livingston!" Claire heard the boss yell from above, her voice muffled but understandable. "You're out of time! Get Bot 3 into position! I've got the frequency narrowed down to within twenty hertz of actual, which should be more than enough!" Her footfalls caused the cellar's ceiling to creak. "Raymond! Fire up the holo-projectors!"

"Right, boss!" came the reply.

Claire didn't know what a holo-whatsit was, but she didn't care to meet any more of these people's magical wonders than she already had. She looked around the basement for something, anything, that might give her an advantage. In the windows, green threads passed by. She had counted on nothing less. In the green light, she saw a lot of nice furniture; the Newsoms had cleaned the cellar up and turned it into living space while she had been away. None of it appeared useful, and it surely weighed a ton to her anyway. She looked up at the ceiling, the walls, and back down to the linoleum floor.

The floor. Floors have drains.

She naturally couldn't fit in the drain. Or could she? Like she could defy gravity and climb on the walls, could she also defy other laws of the living, physical Universe? Maybe she didn't have to physically fit into the drain? Maybe, when she teleported, she wasn't the same size as she normally was? It was worth a shot!

Two concerns hopped into her head. One, did the dome outside extend into the ground? Even if she could travel the length of the pipe in a less-than-corporeal form while she teleported, would she be stopped by a sphere of energy that encased the entire house? Last time that had happened, she had hit it hard, returned to her natural form, and found herself lying on the lawn trying to piece together what had just happened. One thing was certain, she didn't want to find herself in a sewer, or worse yet, in her full form underground. She remembered how hard it had been to dig herself out of only two feet of snow; she had no desire to find out what it might be like to dig her way through possibly ten feet of dirt, back to the surface of the Earth like a common zombie.

And two, where did the pipe lead? She didn't know, and if she didn't know her destination, she couldn't blink there. And what if the end were past the quarter-mile limit? Even if the house allowed her to relocate herself that far, she could re-form in so much pain that she may not have enough wits about her to blink back before the forces-that-be killed her. Permanently. But might that be a better fate than what these ghost hunters had in store for her. Oh, come on, Claire, there must be another—

All thoughts left her mind when the door to the cellar creaked open.

11

The Ghost Hunters,

Part III

Claire held her breath. Was it the humans?

Or the spiders?

With the humans she might have a chance. But as for the spider "bots", as the boss had called them, Claire was becoming deathly afraid, ironic though it sounded. She should blink away right now, she knew, especially if the hunters were smart and had covered the entire floor above her head with those green nets. That's what I would do if I were trying to catch something like me. But maybe they don't have that much green material? If they did, they could have covered the entire ceiling on the second floor with the stuff, and trapped me in the attic!

Unless they didn't want me to stay up there...

Claire tip-toed behind the furnace, and crouched down. Her eyes darted this way and that as she tried to think of a way out. Should she try the drain? The idea of being trapped underground for possibly years as she dug herself out from under the dome didn't sound fun at all. But it was better than being burned alive—even if she was dead—by the spider's green goo. Or worse, sent to The Bad Place... Is there another way?

She heard the now familiar tink, tink-tink of a spider's eight feet.

Great.

A whirring sound accompanied the footsteps, probably its many eyes whirring as they spun in all different directions, looking for her. Not to mention whatever other gadgets were in its disgusting, bulbous body.

Her gaze fell upon something she hadn't seen in years. The little blue pilot light of the central-heating unit glowed between slats in the furnace's metal sheath. Max's family had had such a thing. Pretty ingenious; the furnace was always lit, ready at a moment's notice to fire up and warm the house. How Father would have loved that! She and Mother would have too; it took the fireplace so long to—

The fireplace! Of course!

But had they blanketed it with nets by now? It was worth a shot, at least. And if they had covered it up, she could always teleport back down here to the cellar and try the drain. And then likely be mired deep in the earth until the next century. Possibly spending it in agony if she reappeared too far from the house with no way to quickly claw her way back. Well, like Father used to say, I guess it can't get any worse!

But for both of them, since he had uttered those words, it had gotten worse.

However, at that very moment, either fate sounded better than being cornered by a creepy, mechanical arachnid that shot ghostly acid from its hind-quarters! As if on cue, a glowing green thread sliced her right cheek as it whizzed by. She gasped, blinked away, and was in the living room in a millisecond.

Claire spun around. No one, or more importantly, no thing, was there. She turned to the fireplace, and saw a pretty, glowing web completely covering the wide opening.

Her heart sank, and she dropped to her knees. "Well, the drain it is, then." She shivered at the thought of being buried "alive." She looked up at the fireplace once again, sighed in defeat, and had started to close her eyes to blink into the drainpipe in the cellar, when something caught her attention.

Or rather, the lack of something.

She peered beyond the net, through the fireplace opening, and into the parlor beyond. Two men were in there, busy working on... something. They mumbled words she couldn't make out, but that wasn't important right now. Was she seeing what she thought she saw?

There's no web on the other side!

Could they have missed that? Or might it be a trap? No matter; she was confident she could blink away faster than their bots could net her. She stood up, tip-toed to one of the two closed doors leading to the parlor, if for no other reason than to get a better view of the other side from multiple angles. Satisfied, she blinked up into the flue.

And re-appeared just above the ashes of the large fireplace, staring straight up at a green, glowing net hidden a few feet up. A second later, she landed hard.

NO!

Instinctually, she rolled out of the fireplace and onto the floor of the parlor just as someone yelled, "NOW!" A fresh net blinked into existence over the fireplace, as well as over both doors leading to the living room.

So it was a trap! She pictured the cellar in her mind, and initiated the teleport. But when she opened her eyes, she was still in the parlor. Dear Jesus, no... She stared into three sets of eyes, all staring directly into hers.

* * *

From the parlor's doorway leading to the short hall, Denise marveled at the sight before her. She tucked her smart device away in a pouch on her belt, for she no longer needed it to see ghosts that didn't want to be seen. Not in this amazing room. The holographic projectors not only displayed other-dimensional beings, it also displayed the netting and glowing gridwork her team had installed from floor to ceiling. And by the looks of the little demon's face, it was working. She's trapped.

Thanks to the projectors, Denise could see the little demon as plain as she could see Raymond and Peter. Well, almost. The ghost was still slightly fuzzy and somewhat ill-defined, similar to how it had been on her smart screen in the kitchen. Likely the low resolution of the government equipment, she figured, rather than the limitations of the top-of-the-line holographics of the room.

The ghoul flickered every now and again as it writhed and hissed. It turned its head this way and that, seeming to be looking for an escape rather than deciding on which of her team to attack first. The flickering reminded Denise of an old-time television not perfectly tuned to its station. Or so her grandfather had described it; she had never actually seen a T.V. that had tuning controls in her life.

A wind picked up out of nowhere. The ghost rose into the air, its bony claws spread, its thin, almost skinless arms outstretched to either side of a grotesque mummified skeleton. A severely shredded nightgown, stained with blood, flayed in the powerful wind that grew in intensity with each passing second. Papers and other small debris began to fill the room.

"My God!" Raymond shouted over the growing din. "Would you look at that thing?"

The ghost's skull jerked in the direction of the men, then back to Denise. It now began to float in her direction.

She pulled her special, prototype pistol from her belt and aimed it at the monster before her. "Come on, Claire. Come on and give me a reason to blow you apart!" She raised the blunt weapon with no barrel, and aimed it at the creature's chest. As if the ghost understood—which it surely did on some level—it floated backwards, and hovered near the mantle.

Peter piped up. "Looks like she's been through Hell..."

"At least she's already dressed for where she's headed," added Denise. "Raymond! Why hasn't that bot of yours trapped and cocooned this little devil by now?"

He seemed frozen in place, squinting at the billowing apparition before him.

"Raymond!"

He gawked in Denise's direction. A piece of paper smacked him in the face, but he didn't seem to notice.

"Snap out of it!"

"I've simply never seen one of these things off a phasepanel! It's like... it's like it's real all of a sudden..."

"Raymond!" she hollered. "The bot!"

He blinked. "Oh! Right! Wait, why isn't it—? Oh my God, I forgot to re-engage it after configuring its sensors to the holo-suite!" He fumbled at the spider bot's small screen. "Horace! Charlie! Where are your bots?"

"They're in the cellar!" came Charlie's voice in Denise's earpiece. "They're going through their standard search pattern. Want us to switch to manual?"

"Don't worry about it," Raymond called to them. "I just need a few seconds to get number three here online! It will relay the ghost's new location to the others, and they'll come flying up here faster than you could ever drive them on your own!"

"Roger!" replied Charlie.

Raymond threw a switch and sat back. "Got it!"

Spider Bot 3 sprang into action. Inside two seconds, it attacked. The ghost bounced around the room, easily dodging the glowing webs the spider slung. It tracked her every move, but not fast enough for Denise. It spewed forth plasmatic-web material with a solid four-second pause between threads.

"Raymond, is there any way to speed up that rate of fire?"

"Well, yes," yelled Raymond, as the wind picked up to a gale. "But if I speed up the forming reticulator, it will reduce the tensile strength of the webbing and—"

"Oh enough with the science lesson, just do it!"

"Wilco!"

Denise soon found herself in the throes of a mini-tornado. She protected her face with her hands, and peeked through open fingers to maintain a visual on the demon. Bots 1 and 2 shot into the parlor, plowing right through the green netting because, like Denise and other living beings, they weren't affected by plasmatic material. They took up positions on walls on either side of the room and, working together, targeted the demon zipping to and fro as best they could with the unrefined data that had been programmed into them.

This demon is fast, Denise marveled. Faster than the bots in every way. She is outmaneuvering three bots at once! One second the ghost was on one side of the room, the next second she was on the other. On the ceiling. On the walls. The floor. Back to the ceiling. Her movements caused the projectors to fill the room with a white, ghostly mist, her ratted nightgown leaving a long streak of white haze wherever she went. In seconds, the room looked like a foggy field on a damp morning. She pulled out her meter and switched it back on.

>Beep beep beep<

"Just keep it up a few more seconds, sweetheart," she said under her breath, "and I'll have you."

>Beep beep beep beep<

Denise dodged a green coil that impacted the wall next to her head. Not that the out-of-phase plasma would affect her in any way, but now that they were in a holo-suite and could actually see the stuff sticking to the walls and bricks like overcooked spaghetti, it disgusted her in a way it never had before. She shivered at the thought of any of it clinging, even spiritually, to her seven thousand-dollar Vivica Noir pant suit and her half-length, high-collared synthetic leather jacket.

>Beep beep boooooooooo<

"Got it!" she and Pete yelled together. Denise looked up to see Peter typing away on his smart device.

"Frequency: 6.378 Hertz!" he shouted. "Wavelength: 86.314 nanometers! Energy: 738.41 electron volts!"

Denise smiled. "Bingo, baby." The phrase was something she might never have said had she not loved her grandfather so much, and all the funny little things that used to fly out of his 1970s-born mouth.

A moment later, the wisps of white plasmatic-mist filling the room cleared, and the fuzzy demonic monster bouncing around the room resolved into a pretty, red-headed girl with a pony tail.

Ahh, there you are, Claire.

The bots paused a moment as they received the new data. The ghost seemed to notice something had changed as well, and stopped teleporting for a moment, coming to a rest high in the far corner of the room. Long enough for all three G.I.D.E.O.N.s to aim their abdominal cannons at the same location at the same time, and fire.

The young girl didn't stand a chance.

The glowing ropes of green, plasmatic material found their targets. One wrapped around her left arm, one around her right, the other around her throat. The girl gasped for air as the bots tugged on their web threads. Her hands shot to her throat, and she dropped to the floor in a pile. The tornado died to a gale, then a wind, then finally a breeze. Papers settled to the floor, and the room was calm once more.

G.I.D.E.O.N. 3 climbed over its companions and scurried to where the ghost lay. With its front two legs, it raised her upright and stood her up in the corner. With his hindmost legs it rolled out another long length of glowing thread underneath its body, and in seconds, wrapped the now sweet-looking little demon in a cocoon nearly up to her neck, pinning her arms to her chest. It stood on four legs, its other four legs split between the walls on either side of the ghost girl, balancing its body. Its pincers opened and closed mere inches from her face, ready to snap her head off if told to do so.

Denise ran her fingers through her fine, black hair, which would have been an utterly lost cause; there was a reason she kept it so short. Due to its length in the front, it fell into her eyes as she strode over to Claire.

The ghost pulled the phased-plasma rope away from her neck so she was no longer choking, but her neck was red, and her hands appeared severely burned.

"Ooo," said Denise, "that must hurt."

The girl glared at her.

Denise put her hands on her hips. "Huh! Look at you!" She tilted her head. "You're actually kind of pretty, aren't you? When you're not in your true form, that is."

"True form?" Claire asked. "This is my true form!"

Denise scoffed. "Yeah? It didn't seem so a minute ago, when you still thought you might get away and were trying to terrify us!"

"I didn't change! If you're seeing me differently now, I'm guessing it's because you 'zeroed in on my frequency', or whatever you call it!"

"Hey!" exclaimed Raymond, "we got a smart one this time!"

Denise regarded her. "Yes, she is a bit more 'with it' than most, isn't she? Outsmarted all of us for a good, long while." She bent over and put her face close to the ghost's, just over Bot 3's open mandibles. "Oh my! You have the most amazing emerald eyes! Did anyone ever tell you that?"

The girl looked away.

"Did you have those when you were alive, or are you simply making yourself look like that because that's how you want to see yourself? Your 'residual self-image' as I've heard it called?"

The girl's brow furrowed and she gave Denise a look of confusion.

"Hmm." Denise raised back to her full, six-foot height. "She may be clever, but she has not-a-clue what's really going on. How sad."

* * *

Claire regarded the boss from head to toe. The nasty woman is right about one thing. I don't know what's going on. Not at all. She knew why Daria and Bryan had called these people. There was a ghost in the house, after all! But as non-violent as the Newsoms had been, why hadn't they looked for a nicer way of ridding themselves of her presence? Surely there was a gentle way to allow her to move on, to find her way to the true afterlife? Like where Jonathan had gone? Couldn't they have used a Ouija board or something?

Max had promised her he'd find a way, but he had broken that promise. Maybe not intentionally. Oh, how she longed for Max now. If only she hadn't hurt him. Had he ever forgiven her? Could he ever forgive her? Did he try to keep his promise of finding a way for her to move on? There was no way to know.

What she did know was that she was cocooned by a giant metal spider poised and ready to devour her, hovering right in front of her nose. It "breathed" like a living creature, its body rising and lowering in a steady rhythm, waiting patiently for the command that would allow it to rip her apart. She felt another tear about to drop from her chin, but she was about all cried out. She was moving past fear and onto anger. What are these people waiting on, anyway? If they were going to kill her or send her to Hell or whatever, why hadn't they done it by now? Not that she was complaining. Things simply didn't make sense to her.

Like the parlor. Something was strange about the parlor now. Everyone could see and hear her; it was almost as if she was a living person again. The glowing threads had her trapped like real ropes. She lamented the fact she hadn't figured out the passing-through-walls trick, but she figured it probably wouldn't help her now, anyway. The glowing bands around the house would surely stop her, just like the webs had stopped her from going through the doors or up into the flue.

The boss checked her watch. Was she waiting on something? Mikel, Horace and Charlie stood near the doorway to the short hall now. Claire couldn't remember which was which between Charlie and Horace, but it didn't really matter. Claire was glad to see Mikel seemed no worse for wear. She liked him for some reason. He seemed innocent in all this, somehow.

"You did call them, right?" the boss asked.

"Yes!" said Raymond, then mumbled something.

The woman scowled. "What was that?"

"Twenty minutes ago."

"Only twenty minutes ago?" the steely-eyed woman shouted, with a tone that could peel paint. "If they are yet to fly in from New York, I will absolutely eat your lunch."

Wow, she's that upset and all she's going to do is eat his sandwich? I'd hate to see what she'd do if she gets really mad.

"No, ma'am," said Raymond. "I talked to Terri a couple of hours ago and told them this would be a quick one. Sounded like they're already on their way."

"Sounded like?"

"I can verify."

"You have half a second."

"Yes, boss."

Half a second? Well that already went by. Eat his sandwich! Claire giggled.

The lady spun and locked eyes with her. "You think this is funny, do you?"

Claire lowered her gaze to the floor. To her surprise, the woman's tone lightened.

"I almost want to laugh myself at the absurdity of how things have been going tonight." She turned her head to the side. "Makes me want to scrap every member of this team and start fresh when I get back to the Big Apple."

Claire saw the men around the room give each other looks that were none-too fanciful.

"All except you, darling." This was directed to the one Claire knew to be Peter. "You're stuck with me."

"Only another month, or so my divorce lawyer has promised me."

"We'll see," said the boss, turning back to Claire.

Eww! He married this old witch?

"What are you thinking, little girl?"

Claire realized she must have been making a face without consciously trying to do so.

Peter laughed. "She's probably thinking the same thing I am! 'He married that ol' bag?'"

"You really think I look old?" She made a face of her own, as if she were hurt. "That's ironic, coming from someone who's pushing two hundred!"

These machines didn't allow them to read my mind, too, did they?

"Raymond!" she bellowed, without taking her eyes from Claire. "Any word?"

"Yes, boss!" he replied. "I was right, they're in town. In fact, they should be here any minute."

"Who are they sending?"

"DENISE!" came a bellowing, gruff voice from the hallway.

She closed her eyes, locked her jaw, and let out a slow breath.

"Stand down your blasted bots!" came the voice again.

The boss spun 'round toward the door, and as she did so, she moved just enough for Claire to see around her.

An ancient man with white hair stood with the help of a cane in the doorway next to Horace, Charlie and Mikel. He yelled with surprising authority and volume for his age, and held up a glowing rectangle with words and numbers flashing over its surface. "I've got a point-order directive. Straight from Callahan!"

That voice sounds familiar and not familiar at the same time.

The boss scoffed. "It figures they sent you to finish this particular exorcism. Talked 'em into one final mission, eh, Max?"

Claire was unable to move any of her limbs, but it didn't stop her jaw from hitting the floor. She studied his face for any sign of recognition.

"No one's being exorcised tonight," said the old man. "Stand down your men and spiders. Now, Mrs. Livingston!" He looked at Claire, locked eyes with her a moment, then smiled.

It is Max! My Max!

Denise strode across the parlor to him, and yanked the glowing rectangle from his hand. "Well at least you got the name right." She studied the document for a moment, then shoved it back at him.

"Bot 3, pause! And station!" she called over her shoulder.

The men around the room groaned collectively, and the spider climbed off Claire and lowered itself to the floor in front of her. It still looked menacing, but at least it no longer seemed as though it was about to eat her.

"Terri talked Callahan into this, didn't she?" Denise said through clenched teeth, "Because I know it wasn't all you. When I get back to New York, the first thing I'm going to do is fire that girl! No! The first thing I'm going to do is make her feel an inch tall for her utter disloyalty. The second thing I'm going to do is toss her out on her—"

"Good! Do it! Then she can join a team with a leader who applauds her for doing what is morally right, instead of punishing her for it!"

"And what am I doing that is so wrong? Honestly, Max! Tell me!"

"We really need to go over it again?"

"If I'm breaking department policy or the law, have the MPs fly out here and arrest me! Or is that what you're doing? Are they waiting outside? Is Callahan waiting in the wings to swallow the key to my cell?"

"Denise, I'm telling you, the days of the Exorcism and Eradication teams are numbered. Callahan and the entire board now agree these may not be the best means to—"

"Oh, spare me!" Denise turned her back to him. "I've read your paper. 'Exodus: A Less-Lethal Means of Ghost Busting'. Give me a break. As if any of it even matters."

"It matters to the ghosts."

"What, they have rights now?" Denise said, motioning to Claire. "Under the law? Since when? Since I left the office yesterday?"

"Of course not. But they're human beings—"

"Were human beings. They're nothing but imprints now. Copies of their former selves. Nothing about them is human anymore. If any of them ever was!"

"You don't know any of that for a fact."

"Neither do you!"

The room fell silent.

Claire looked down at herself. I'm a... a copy?

"All I know is you've got a sweet little girl cocooned in a corner," Max shouted, "terrified out of her mind that she's about to be devoured by a giant, mechanical spider!"

"A sweet little girl?" Denise yelled, towering over Max's frail frame. "Did you even read the dozens of reports on this house?"

"Every one," he said. "Even wrote a few of them."

"Yes, we all know you used to live here. And so you should know better than anyone this 'girl' was anything but sweet! In your own sister's words—"

"She retracted that report," Max spat.

"Too late! It was in the public domain on the Internet, and had made it into our system. Her account, combined with all the others..." Denise shook her head. "No, Max, this little demon was anything but sweet."

Claire's shoulders would have slumped, had she room inside her cocoon to do so. I'm finally going to pay for my sins, just like Mother and Pastor Phillip said we all would eventually. I'm going to pay with my soul.

"She finally did the same thing to you as she did your sister, and yet you're still in love with her and want to save her."

Max's gaze shot back to Denise, and he spoke in a quiet voice. "I told you that in confidence. Back when we could call ourselves friends. Back when we both agreed this house would remain on 'exempt' status until such time as the Committee made a decision regarding the Exodus Program. My feelings toward this girl are inadmissible here."

He still loves me. Max still loves me!

"You're probably right. I've already tried to get Callahan to relieve you based on your personal feelings toward ghosts, this particular one especially—making you scientifically un-biased toward the program—but he won't listen. Sometimes I honestly think he's on your side. But no matter; your morbid devotion to this 'girl' will not help sway the Committee to ban all exorcisms and eradications."

"I'm sorry," Claire whispered. "For everything I did."

Max pursed his lips and closed his eyes.

"For now," Denise went on to say, "you win, Max. You got your point-order. Congratulations. But I'm afraid you've won yet another battle, but lost the war itself. The Board can order exodus over exorcism in 'Gray Cases' such as this one all they want. In fact, when you think about it, it's silly of me to even want them to stop! Silly of me to demand exorcisms and eradications across the board! Why would I do such a thing? Talk about putting myself out of a job! I have complete job security your way! Sending a ghost away to haunt another day somewhere else? You'd think that would be all we

do; it would keep us in business indefinitely! Right?
So why do I take the stance I do if it means I'm
putting myself out of a job?"

Max said nothing. He seemed to know what was
coming.

"Even if people didn't continue to be born and die
and keep us in business, I would still do whatever I
can to eliminate every evil entity from this world!
Unless you, Mr. Genius, can not only find a way to
un-imprint a ghost from a location and send it on its
way to Heaven or Hell, but prevent a soul facsimile
from occurring in the first place, we'll hunt specters
until the sun burns out! Are you working on
something like that?"

Max shook his head. "No. And you know there's
not even any proof—"

"Does it matter whether there's proof or not?"
Denise asked. "Ghosts exist, no matter the reason!
The government knows it, and the whole world will
know soon, if I have any say in the matter!" She
stepped closer to him. "We didn't invent the things,
Max. They've been here since life began roaming the
Earth. God apparently wants it that way because
He's allowed it to happen. And everything's just fine
until they start upsetting the living. That's where our
department comes in, Max. We're here to allow
good people to continue to live happy lives, in their
homes, on their lands, in their space stations and
wherever the department sends us. I've already got
my bags packed and ready for my first trip to Mars!"

Max took a deep breath. "Denise, I readily admit
we still don't know exactly what's going on here." He

motioned to Claire. "That apparition right there, it could be merely a facsimile of Claire Harvey. Or it could be the Claire Harvey. The original. Either trapped here against her will, or unable to leave simply because she doesn't know how. She doesn't want to be here, believe me! She would much rather move on. But she can't. All I want to do is give her the chance to do so. And beyond that, I want to be granted enough time for the proper research to be done to prove I'm right. To prove that that really is Claire Harvey wrapped up in your cocoon, and every ghost we've ever encountered actually was the person they were in life!"

Denise smiled. "Well, it looks like you're going to get at least one of those things; she's going to get her chance. You've got your point-order. Go ahead! Set her free! It's just one more ghost for us to be paid to catch again."

Yes! Set me free!

She turned to Claire. "Just pick someplace tropical next time, hmm? I could use a trip to the Mediterranean, if you don't mind."

"See?" said Max. "That's the spirit! No pun intended." He chuckled at his own joke. "Now, is it really the end of the world?" He lifted his chin toward Raymond. "Let her go."

Denise's gaze turned hard and she lowered her voice. "It could be someday. Absolutely and without question it could be the end of the world. These... these ethereal beings, they don't need to be roaming around here among the living, causing havoc and destruction and terror! Thinking that they still have a claim to the places they haunt! Thinking they're still human. Or ever were in the first place! These demons—and believe me, that's exactly what they are, demons—need to be sent back to Hell where they belong. Sent back to Hell in our exorcisms or destroyed altogether in our eradications! God isn't against it, otherwise priests would never have been able to do such a thing in the first place! He wants us here, doing our jobs!"

"I doubt the God of the Hebrews ever intended a government organization calling itself the Department of Paranormal Affairs to capture a soul, pass judgment, and send His children to Hell all on its own," Max countered. "Aren't we bypassing the system He himself set up? What does your Holy Bible say about that?"

The volume of her voice dropped once again. "I'll tell you one thing He never intended. He never intended for humans to consort with them. It's nothing more than outright self-condemnation! You have consorted with this demon all your life, and now, because you're in love with it, you now believe it and every evil thing like it should have rights like a human! Are you so blind you can't see how disgusting that is, for Chrissakes?"

"Careful now," Max muttered, "you wouldn't want to blaspheme, would you?"

Her whole body shook. "Are you so deaf you can't hear the blasphemy coming out of your own mouth?" she screamed. "Soulless creatures like you should be removed from God's Green Earth!" And with that, she jerked her arm up and pointed her blunt weapon directly at Max's chest.

"Denise!" shouted Raymond.

Oh my dear God in Heaven! The anger flared within Claire as she struggled with the ropes that held her fast.

Max held up his hand, the with the court-order now dangling between two fingers, the others outstretched. "It's alright, everyone, it's alright!" He spun carefully on his cane to address the others in the room.

Claire gritted her teeth, screamed out, and managed to rip two strands of rope, freeing one hand.

"Bot 3, contain!" Denise shouted.

The spider rose on its haunches and fired a net that encompassed Claire's chest and midsection, pinning her against the wall.

"No!" Claire yelled. She struggled and pushed with all her might.

Max's brows shot up. "It's okay, Claire, it's okay," he said in a calming voice. "Please calm down. It will be okay."

Claire hyperventilated. She kept struggling but was now cocooned more tightly than before. With a single motion, the bot had effectively eliminated any further chance of escape. She sighed. "Max! Max, I'm sorry!"

"It's alright, everyone's cool. Calm and cool... Just everyone stay put and give me a minute here." He turned back to the boss. "So, Denise, the truth finally rears its ugly head."

The boss set her jaw and towered above him. Her hands shook under the influence of the adrenaline coursing through her. A blood vessel in her forehead looked as though it might burst at any moment. "Get out," she said in a level tone.

Max's gaze shifted between her, the court order, and back to her again. "You know I can't do that."

"Oh, yes you can," she replied. "Just turn and walk out that door, and let me finish the job."

"Our boss signed this order. This little ghost is not worth the administrative punishment that will fall upon you if you ignore it. Let my team finish up here."

"I'm not going to let you get away with another exodus!" Even her voice was shaky now. "Point-order be damned. Ray, reprogram the Rainbow Bridge. We're not performing an exorcism anymore. Set it to eradication."

Claire's eyes grew ten sizes. She watched every set of eyes in the room bounce among the others.

"Boss?" asked Ray.

"Do as you're told," she said, keeping her eyes on Max.

"But, boss..." Ray stumbled over his words. "Boss, it's a point-order. We'll all be reprimanded. If not let go!"

"You will not be let go! You will have simply been following orders given by your Team Lead. I will assume responsibility! Now do as I say if you want to keep your paychecks!" she screamed.

The men looked at Max, who shook his head.

Denise whirled on her men. "I am your Team Lead! Not Max Butler! And I have given you a command! You will heed it or I will ensure each of you is terminated from federal service! Good luck getting another job that doesn't include a paper hat!"

Max took two steps forward, and leaned into the gun.

Claire could see it pressing into his three-piece suit, directly at his heart. She wanted to close her eyes and blink away, but even if she could, she couldn't leave the soul she loved to this fate. Instead she settled on crying.

"Raymond," Max called over his shoulder, never taking his eyes from Denise, "you can do as she says. But just know that if you do, you will have to stand before a Board of Inquiry and explain why you disregarded an order signed by the Director himself! And explain why you saw fit to permanently destroy what could someday be proven to be a sentient human being with a soul, and not simply a facsimile as she claims!" He then addressed Denise. "What would your church say, if ghosts like Claire turn out to be people merely stuck between worlds? People who only need a little help to find their way? Or would your church even believe the scientific evidence laid out before them?"

"As if you have any evidence. Or ever will."

"We don't yet," admitted Max, "but we're getting there. At the very least, I can buy some time with exoduses, and allow these entities to escape the places they've imprinted upon, or simply show them the path to freedom. Allow the families affected to move on with their lives without being haunted by the ghosts stuck in their homes, most of whom don't really want to be there in the first place."

Denise snarled, and raised the gun to a point just below his chin. "Some of them want to be there. Some of them love to torture the living."

Claire took as deep a breath as she could manage inside the cocoon, and looked away. I'm guilty. I'm guilty of what she says. They all know it. Especially Max.

"Yes," said Max softly, "some of them do enjoy the hauntings."

My soul is doomed. As it should be. I really am evil.

"And we'll deal with those difficult souls as we come across them," he said. "But Claire isn't one of those."

Claire looked up. What?

He turned to face her. "Are you, Claire?"

She looked around. All eyes in the room were upon her.

Max scoffed. "Of course she's not. We can set her free with no ill consequence, and allow my section to continue its work. Denise, don't let the fear and hatred in your heart make you do what you surely know is wrong. When you exorcise these ghosts, you're sending them to a terrible place, which could easily be the Hell you believe in. At that moment, they are in both worlds, ours and their new destination, and the look on every ghost's face right before he or she is exorcised tells us it's a terrible, unthinkable fate that awaits them. And when we eradicate them, we are almost certainly killing them permanently."

"Max!" Denise laughed, her voice raising an octave, "they're already DEAD!"

"Just their physical bodies are dead. Their soul lives on even after death! Your religion tells you that, yes?" Max grabbed her by both arms, still expertly maintaining control of his cane. "You destroy those souls with each eradication, Denise. You're erasing them from existence! You're doing more damage each time you do it—sinning in God's eyes more completely—than even a murderer does here on Earth! Should any human have the power to do such a thing? Condemn a soul to oblivion?"

Her breath caught in her throat, and she stared at Max a long moment. "You're trying to twist my words and confuse me!" She shook her head. "No! That's not true! You can't prove that's what we're doing! You can't prove these things are people! You can't prove they're not demons!"

"Not yet. But what if I do?"

"You won't! I'll make sure of that! I'll personally ensure your section is shut down and all your work is destroyed!"

"You could try. But even if you succeed, I could still be right, couldn't I? We could all die in the next five minutes, but all our souls will still exist, won't they? They'll head off to the Pearly Gates for judgment, isn't that right? And what will God say if I'm right?"

Tears ran down Denise's cheeks now.

Clare stared on, incredulous. *Keep on her, Max! I think you're actually getting through her thick skull!*

"You were involved in the development and testing of our equipment. Our own tests tell us that once an eradication is performed, there is no trace of the ghost that was there. And why? Because it's deleted from existence; you've eradicated it from the Universe. And if there's the slightest chance it was indeed a person, and not merely a copy of one, or not a demon from the fiery pit of Hell, you're responsible for committing well beyond the act of murder, Denise. You have destroyed something that God himself created. If that's not an abomination, I don't know what is."

"No!" Denise yelled, shaking her head. "I don't believe it. I refuse to believe it! He wouldn't allow me to have that kind of power!"

"But what if He does? Just as He eventually allowed us to build skyscrapers, when He once destroyed the Tower of Babel? He allows us the ability to fly. To travel through space and explore the Heavens. To split the atom! What if He allows us to have all this knowledge and acquire these powers, merely to see if we will use them properly? And avoid the temptation to use them for evil?"

"This isn't a test!"

"God tested many people in your holy book, Denise. Is it so hard to believe He could be testing you as well?"

Wait. Claire's gaze darted about. Could God have been testing me this entire time? To see if I could avoid temptation? Avoid evil? If so, have I failed in His eyes?

"You're trying to turn my religion against me. You're a disbeliever trying to tell me what the Bible says! Only Satan would do that!"

"Satan?"

"Any lover of demons is in league with Satan! You, my old friend, are a tool of evil! The very evil you're trying to twist around and lay upon me! It won't work, Max! God sees through your deceit!"

"Will you listen to yourself? You're succumbing to fantasy and madness! I'm not an agent of evil, I'm trying to open your eyes to the truth!"

"The truth!" she spat. "Who are you to dictate what is true and what is not? You're merely a man! A frail, fallible human being, just like everyone else! You don't speak to God as I do! As Father Benjamin does! You don't know what I know!"

"I know you're leaving this house," Max said.

"I will do no such thing." Denise seemed to grow taller than she was even a moment ago. She spread her arms wide, the gun now pointing in Claire's direction. "I am on the side of Right and Righteousness! I have the moral high ground! I am not subject to the immoral orders of man! I answer to a power greater than Director Callahan, greater than the Board, greater than the Department of Paranormal Affairs, greater even than the United States Constitution!"

Claire's eyes followed the strange gun wherever it went. Don't accidentally pull the trigger... Don't accidentally pull the trigger...

"They will not destroy my resolve!" Denise continued. "God will stand by my side! He will forgive me if I destroy a few souls in the war against Satan himself! I am a warrior of the Almighty—we all are, every man on my team—sent to protect the human race from Darkness! Commissioned and entrusted with sending these demons back to where they belong, and allowing good, innocent people to pursue peace and happiness and the pure love of Jesus Christ, without fear from the hauntings these abominations bring into their lives!" She now pointed the gun casually at Raymond, whose eyes doubled in size. "Now follow my orders, Mr. Parker!" She then swept the gun back in Claire's direction, as if she had forgotten it was in her hand and was merely pointing a harmless finger. "You will not send that thing back to Hell, Raymond, you will erase it from existence! Re-program the Bridge! Configure it for Oblivion."

No one moved.

Max nodded. "I was afraid you wouldn't see reason, Denise." He touched his ear. "Boys, I've done all I can do."

Claire heard the front door burst open, and the sound of an army approaching echoed in the foyer. Within seconds, six men dressed all in black flooded the room, pointing nasty looking black sticks at everyone except Max.

"Woah, woah, woah!" Mikel shouted, and bumped into Horace in his attempt to move back from the approaching soldiers.

Raymond and Charlie backed away as well. "Hey, easy!" shouted Raymond.

"Now, boys," said Pete, hands in front him, "let's not be gettin' no itchy trigger fingers, now."

"Get your hands where I can see them!" one of the soldiers announced.

Every man's hands and arms shot high into the air. Two soldiers moved toward Claire and pointed boxy looking things similar to Denise's blunt weapon at her.

"They won't hurt you, sweetheart." Max gave Claire a look that meant business. "As long as you don't move."

She looked down at the glowing cocoon. "Like I could if I wanted to!"

"Just... don't pull any tricks, okay?"

She eyed the soldiers pointing those strange, possibly soul-stealing guns at her head. Every instinct told her to flee. She trusted Max, but *can I trust him with my soul?* She knew the answer to that question before it had even fully formed in her mind. *Absolutely.* "Okay," she agreed. "No tricks, Max."

He winked.

"You can stay exactly as you are, Ms. Bixby," said the soldier who'd spoken a moment ago. "Just let the pistol fall to the ground."

Denise looked down at herself, seeming to only now realize both her arms were outstretched, her palms pointed skyward, and a weapon had somehow found its way into her hand. "It's Livingston." She let the pistol fall. As soon as it made a solid thud upon the wooden floor, the soldier was upon her, zip-tying her hands behind her back.

"It's Bixby!" Pete Livingston called from across the room. "I will not be associated with that crazy ol' coot!"

Denise turned and faced Max, her jaw clenched. "I should have known you would pull something like this. You coward." She spat the word in his face. "Look at you, old man. You don't even have the guts to stand up to me and see your convictions through."

"Oh, I think I stood up to you nicely," said Max, stepping over to Raymond's equipment and punching buttons. "But you're right, I am a very old man, and my body isn't as keen as it once was." He looked around at the soldiers. "We all need a little help from our friends once in a while, don't we? You have Father Benjamin and your congregation. I have the U.S. Army Special Forces. Luckily for everyone involved, the Department of Paranormal Affairs puts a little more faith in its fifty-year veteran operatives than it does in its fifteen-year religious zealots." He threw one final switch, and the glowing cocoon around Claire dissolved, along with every glowing thread and web in the room. The green glow was gone, replaced once again by the soft light of the lamps mounted on the dark walls.

Claire fell to the floor. She could breathe again!

Max hobbled to her side, and knelt down beside her. "Are you alright?"

She nodded. "I'm fine."

"I'm not so sure..." He looked down at her arms.

It was then Claire noticed her hands and arms were covered in burns, some of them severe. "Oh no."

"Don't worry, sweetheart. Soon you won't have to worry about any of this anymore."

"Wait," said Raymond, who was the last to be zip-tied, "can they do this? Are we being arrested? I know my rights! I wanna talk to my lawyer!"

"Relax, Raymond, you're not being held prisoner," Max assured him.

"Sir, we're ready here," said the soldier who appeared to be in charge, and all eyes fell upon Max.

"Just a moment, Lieutenant." Max leaned on his cane, and climbed slowly and deliberately to his feet. "Listen, friends, you're only being escorted out to your vehicles. These men will see to it you retrieve all your belongings from your hotel, and then make sure you get on your plane back to New York. Tonight. Then you'll never see them again, I promise. Oh, and I've been directed to tell you all that you are to report to the main office as soon as you get back for debriefing, no matter the hour. Mr. Callahan will be waiting to debrief you himself."

"Mr. Callahan?" asked Raymond.

"He's been watching and listening this entire time." Max touched the frame of his glasses. "None of you have anything to worry about, you all performed as per your ethics and morality training to a tee." He turned to the tallest person in the room, even taller than the soldiers. "However, you, Denise, might find yourself in a different situation. And you might find yourself something of a celebrity when the media gets a hold of this. Not sure if it will be fame or infamy, though. Time will tell, I suppose. And Mr. Parker, don't worry, I'll make sure all your equipment makes it back to your lab safe and sound." He turned back to Denise. "You see? I'm not a monster, after all."

"No," said Denise. "You're much worse." She looked over to Claire. "You're a man in love."

The lieutenant raised one arm and made a gesture. "Alright, Team Lima, let's go."

A soldier pulled Denise by the arm and ushered her toward the door.

Pete raised his eyebrows as Denise passed by him. "Bit much, wouldn't you say, Love?"

Denise smiled, winked, and shot a kiss in his direction.

"Eww," Claire said under her breath.

Once Denise was through the short hallway, her still-commanding voice echoed off the hard surfaces of the foyer. "The fate of the future is in your hands, Director Callahan! And the blood of everyone on Earth is on yours, Max Butler! Only Satan himself will be judged more harshly than you!"

There were more crazy mumblings, but Claire couldn't make them out. She was thankful for that.

The room emptied, leaving Max and Claire alone. Alone for the first time in over sixty years. His eyes found hers, and he held out his hands. "My sweet, darling Claire."

In the blink of an eye she was upon him, squeezing him with every ounce of strength she had left after this ordeal. The tears filling her eyes blurred everything around her.

He sucked in a quick breath and seemed to gasp. "Oh!" Claire broke the embrace. "Did I hurt you?"

Max smiled. "No my dear, I guess I had forgotten how cold it could get when we did that."

"Oh, I'm so sorry!"

"It's fine, I'm fine. These old bones simply chill more easily than they used to."

"Max... Thank you for coming back for me."

"I made a promise to you, Claire. I wasn't about to break it."

She hugged him again, just a little tighter, but more carefully this time.

"I've missed you, sweetheart. I've missed you so much."

Tears streamed down her face. "You can't begin to know how much I've missed you! I thought I'd never see you again because you hated me."

"Hated you?" Max asked, breaking the hug. He put his face close to hers. "How could I ever hate you?"

"After what I did to you—"

"Love makes us do crazy things sometimes."

Claire chuckled, and wiped a tear from her face. "It does, doesn't it?"

"You were upset with the situation, at me having to leave, not at me personally. I'll admit, it took me a lot of years to understand that, but when I did, I forgave you completely and unconditionally. I focused even more on keeping my promise."

"But why didn't you ever come and see me?"

Max took a deep breath. "Like I said, it took me a lot of years to understand and forgive you, and not be afraid of you. When it finally happened, well, too much time had passed. I didn't know what to say to you. I didn't know if you'd forgive me for acting the way I did all those years."

"Oh, Max." Claire shook her head.

"And then when I came into this room and saw you for the first time after all these decades, I was that ten-year-old kid all over again. It doesn't help that you look exactly the same as you did the first day I remember seeing you. You're just as lovely now as you always were. As you always will be." He shook his head. "But me, I must look hideous to you!"

"What? You could never look hideous to me! You're my knight in shining armor! You came back and saved me! I will always love the soul inside you, no matter what you look like on the outside. How could I not? You did the same for me all your life."

"Well, that's not entirely true. I never saw you as the ghoulish, decomposing apparition everyone else seemed to. Whenever I saw you, you were always a gorgeous young lady, both inside and out."

"Not everyone saw me as the decrepit monster. Your father saw me as you do."

"You met my father?"

"I was there when he died. I was at his bedside just as you and Sophie were."

"You were there? But I didn't see you!"

"I know. I made sure of that. I didn't want to upset you. Sophie told me about your wife and family."

"Sophie!"

"It's okay, Max! Really. She and I talked everything out. We're fine now. And she enlightened me on things. About you. About Miranda. It was for the best I stayed away."

Max's pupils shifted from side to side, as if he was trying to put all the pieces together.

"I did it for your marriage. For your family. For you."

He closed his eyes and a tear streamed down his wrinkled, sunken cheek.

"How is Sophie?" Claire asked. She leaned over to peer into the foyer for a hint of another person. "She didn't happen to come with you on this momentous occasion, did she?"

Max lowered his head. "Sophie passed on eight years ago, Claire. The cancer finally took her. Just like it took Mom."

A tear dropped from her chin. "Oh, no! Oh, Max, I'm so sorry."

"I miss her. That cranky old windbag!"

Claire couldn't help but chuckle. She hugged him again. She would have climbed inside him had she the ability.

Behind Max, the hands of the large transparent clock hovering above the mantle were positioned at Nine-Forty-Two. She now had time to read the fancy yellow letters below it. "9:42 PM 27 JUNE 2061."

2061? Well that means Max must be—

"I miss Miranda, too," he continued, interrupting her math. "She left this world not long after Sophie. Her artificial heart did the best it could. Probably

gave her twenty more years of life. But in the end...
It simply couldn't keep up."

Claire dug her face into the old man's collar. "I'm
so sorry. I didn't know."

"It's okay, Claire. You couldn't have known." He
pulled away, and shivered slightly. He looked at her
and smiled. "Hey, ninety three years is a nice, long
life. She had no regrets. I only wish the Good Lord or
Death or whomever would finally come on and take
me. I made it to my goal; I saw Halley's Comet for
the second time in my life! I'm about done now."

"Done? No, Max, you still have work left to do!"
She took his hands in hers. "You're fighting the good
fight! God's not going to take you while there are
still souls left to be saved from crazies like Denise!
I'm not a copy of Claire Harvey! And I'm not a
demon!"

His shoulders fell. "Of course you're not, Claire.
But I'm not the only person on my team. There are
several others who can take up the fight, and who
will continue my work smashingly when I'm no
longer around. Sweetie, I really don't want to live to
be so decrepit I can't even get around."

"But you get around just fine."

"Yeah, as long as I have my trusty third leg!" He
tapped his cane on the hardwood floor. "Thankfully,
my hip is about the only thing wrong with me. My
doctor says I'm so healthy, I could live to be a
million! Okay, maybe not a million..."

Claire laughed at the joke; she had almost
forgotten how she'd used to exaggerate everything.

A voice rang out in the room. "Um, Max?"

Max froze.

Claire looked around, trying to figure out where the voice came from. "Who was that?"

Max then cleared his throat. "Uh, yes! Veronica, is that you?"

"Yes, Max," the voice rang out again, in a sweet, almost teasing tone. "Did you forget we're all still here? We've been watching and listening to everything you two say. Thomas here is getting a little bleary eyed, so I thought we'd better wrap this up soon." She sniffled after her last word.

"Oh!" he exclaimed. "Yes, of course! Sorry!"

"It's okay. We wanted to give you some time, we all know this is a big moment. But Max, it will be the witching hour before we're out of here tonight, and we all know you need your ten hours of beauty sleep, or else you turn into Mr. Cranky-Butt Butler."

Max shook his head. "Of course, of course! Please come in!"

Claire's brows came together. "Max?"

"It's okay, sweetheart. My friends are going to make sure you get on your way."

Her mouth fell open. "Really? You can really do that?"

"Of course! I wasn't saying all those things to hear my head rattle."

"I won't have to be stuck in this house? On this property? I will be able to go wherever I want?"

"Wherever you want."

Claire squealed, hugged Max a fourth time, and jumped up and down.

"Careful, my dear! Careful! My bones!"

She stopped. "Oh, I'm so sorry again! But yay!" She stepped back and continued bouncing up and down until people streamed into the room.

There were seven in all. Each one seemed taken aback upon seeing her in the light of the projectors. Some of them smiled, and to those, she smiled back. She couldn't help herself. She didn't know what they were going to do, but she trusted Max one-hundred percent.

She would be free. Free from the bonds of the old house on Hollow Street.

Max took a seat in one of the chairs and seemed content to let the crew do its work. He reached into his pocket and pulled out a pipe.

"So, you smoke now?" Claire asked.

"Not exactly."

Smoke wafted upward, but it dissipated quickly. Claire examined it. "Is that not smoke?"

"It's water vapor."

A scent reached Claire. "Hey! I can actually smell that!"

"I would have guessed you can see, hear, and smell everything about me," said Max. "Our studies show that living people as well as objects can become 'belongings' to a ghost, if enough interaction takes place between them. I suspected I'm probably one of your 'belongings', after everything we've been through together."

That made her smile.

The new team used Raymond's equipment, plus a few strange boxes and devices of their own. Not that Claire understood any of the technical babble that flew about the room, but she did understand they were modifying it not to "eradicate" her—which would apparently kill her permanently—nor to send her to the fiery pit of Hell, but to free her from her captivity. Grant her "exodus", as Max and Denise had called it. Like Moses led his people out of Egypt and toward freedom, so Max will lead me out of my entrapment and toward my own Promised Land. See, Mother? I remembered something from the Bible! "Um, Max?"

"Yes, Claire?"

"Is this going to be quick, or—?"

"Why, do you have someplace to be? Perhaps a hot date with the ghost down the street?"

She made a face. "The thin man? No! Gross!"

"Something on TV?"

"No, Max."

"Then what does it matter?"

She shrugged. "It doesn't, I was just curious. But hey, speaking of the neighbor—"

"I've already got a team on it. And let me tell you, there are a whole lot of families that will be happy when that exodus is completed!"

"So he's still there? But Old Man Moody's house was torn down. I thought maybe he was freed—"

"It's not the house that has kept him tied to his earthly residence. Just like this house isn't what's been keeping you here."

"No?"

"No, Claire," said Max. "But I can see why you might think that. And I've done what I could to protect this house and its property until I could conduct your exodus. Not because it's my childhood home—although that was a bonus—but because I wanted to make things less traumatic and aggravating for you. This was, is, your home just as it was once mine. You can move around in it, interact with things, feel safe here. The thin man, he lost his home. And unless he gets extremely frustrated and angry, he can't interact with anything in his haunt radius. Like I said, he's been causing quite a stir in the last few years."

"So, if it's not the house..."

"Claire, you are what's keeping you here. Your connection with this life. Your inability to fully let go and move on. We're going to show you how to finally let go."

* * *

An hour later, the preparations were complete. Claire fidgeted in one of the comfy chairs in the parlor, hoping she understood everything she had been taught. The moment of truth would be upon her, as soon as "the calibrations were complete." At least that's what a technician had said a moment ago.

Max stared at her from the other comfy chair and puffed on his pipe. "You made all this possible, Claire."

Her brows came together. "Me? How on Earth could—?"

"You were the inspiration for my interest in math and science. I hated it. All of it. But you had a way of explaining each problem I came across in simple terms a boy of seven, ten, twelve, thirteen could understand. You showed me how to look at complex problems in a different way, with all the patience in the world."

"With eyes from a simpler time. And of course I was patient. It's not like I was a normal teenager and had somewhere else to—"

"Don't ruin this."

She lowered her head and smiled. "Okay."

"See," Max continued, "if you hadn't tutored me, Claire, I don't know where I'd be right now. And you, well..."

"I'd be in Hell right now. If I still existed at all."

He nodded. "The ghost hunters would have come eventually, regardless. It may have been a hundred years from now, or two, but someone would have eventually figured out all my science, whether I had been part of the research and development or not."

"I'm glad you were."

"Me too. This way, you have a third option. A way out."

"So that entire time I was helping that little boy with his homework, I was saving myself, my soul, and didn't even know it."

Max closed his eyes and nodded.

"The Universe works in mysterious ways just like God, huh?"

"Always has," Max agreed. "Some of us believe the two are one and the same." Max took another puff of his pipe, and checked a display not far from his chair.

Claire looked over at the big orange box in which Max's team had tucked away Denise's gun for safe return back to the Department of Paranormal Affairs. "Max, I have a question."

"Shoot."

"Ha, funny you should reply like that, because I was just thinking... That gun Denise had. It was a 'ghost gun' wasn't it?"

"Yes. A phased-plasma-stream pistol. It's a mouthful, I know." He chuckled. "I named it."

"So, it couldn't have actually hurt anyone in this room but me, right? But if that were the case, why didn't you just take it away from her?"

"And blow her delusions of grandeur out of the water? No, I had things completely under control the way it was. When possibly violent people believe they are in control, everyone can have a nice, quiet discussion. Had she become desperate, there's no telling what she might have done. She might have instructed those bots to—" Max cut himself off. "Well, they could have really hurt you, Claire. I couldn't risk that."

Claire nodded. The mere thought of what those mechanical nasties could have done sent a shiver through her from head to toe.

"But actually, now that you mention it," Max went on to say, stroking his stubbly chin, "Denise's pistol is a prototype..." He shifted in his seat. "You see, against my better judgment, she had that thing boosted to eleven milliamps, giving it quite a punch over any of our other 'ghost' weapons. If the internal magnetron isn't calibrated just right, even though it's out-of-phase with the living, it still could have knocked over a guy the size of Raymond, and likely have stopped my heart before I hit the floor."

"Oh my goodness!"

"But I was more worried about you! One blast could have blown one of your arms or legs off, my dear Claire, and I mean permanently!" He shook his head. "What it might have done had it hit somewhere else..." His voice trailed off.

The glare she bore into the side of Max's head could have punched a hole through steel.

"But I don't think even Denise had it in her to pull that trigger," Max said. "She knew where the line was drawn, whether she wanted to admit it or not. I'm just glad you didn't attack her! She may have then had a reason to use that heinous weapon against you, then plead self-defense during the resulting Board of Inquiry. Don't worry, I'll see that it's disassembled when we return to New York."

"Sir?" said one of the technicians. "We're ready."

"Please begin," Max acknowledged.

Claire grabbed his arm, preventing him from standing up.

"Sweetheart? What's the matter?"

"I'm scared."

"You have nothing to be frightened of."

"But aren't there ghosts, well, everywhere out there?"

"Yes, as a matter of fact, there are."

"But what if they...? I mean... I don't have any way to protect myself! I don't have a cross, I don't have one of Denise's guns, I don't have you—"

"Claire, calm down. You have the power of Apparitic Relocation. What you used to call 'blinking away'. With that power, you can escape any situation, any danger."

"Teleportation."

"That's right!" he said, smiling big. "You've learned a thing or two!"

"But how does that help me? Don't all ghosts have this same power?"

"Many do," Max admitted. "But I promise you, teleportation is the most powerful superpower of all. Outside of the ability to stop time, that is."

"But, doesn't that mean a fiendish ghoul could chase me just as fast as I could run?"

"They have to figure out where you're going, first!"

Claire furrowed her brow. "Well it wouldn't be all that hard to find me; I can go to Heaven, come back to Earth, maybe visit Baltimore finally, go back to Heaven... Am I missing something, here?"

"Claire, listen. Once the imprint is broken, and you cross-over properly, all limits are off. You can not only travel past the 400-meter prohibitive barrier that's kept you here so long, but a spirit properly tuned to the Universe's frequency can blink away to any single point anywhere within her. Your distance is, as far as we can tell, unlimited. Heaven, the Heavens, the Universe, whatever you want to call it, is vast beyond imagination. It would take an eternity to locate someone who didn't want to be found.

"And that's just the tip of the iceberg," Max went on to say. "We've learned a lot from other ghosts who we've set free from the chains that bound them. Some of them return and communicate with us regularly. Help us further our research. Not only can many ghosts travel to the ends of the Universe, some have reported that they can reach any time period they wish."

"Any... Time?"

The old man nodded once. "As well as other planes of existence. And there is surely so much more we don't know. That we can't know. That only people like you can find, once you're on the Other Side."

"Oh Max, I don't understand any of this!"

He laughed and stood up. "I have a feeling you'll figure it out. Just explore, sweetheart. The rest will come."

She was directed to stand in the center of the room, on a platform that shone with all the colors of the rainbow and beyond; the "Rainbow Bridge" Denise had mentioned. Her mind was awash with possibilities, and one serious concern. "Max, how will I find you once I leave this place? I've never been to your home or your office or anything. And how will we find each other, once you, um, you know..."

Max took her hands in his. "As I understand it, many of the rules you have had to endure these last hundred and sixty years change once we perform this procedure. Once you're free."

"But—

"Stop worrying, Claire. You and I, my dear, we're bound by the strongest bond there is. Simply close

your eyes, and think of me. The Universe will show
you the way."

12

Unending

Max is hurting.

Claire reached her mind out, across the Heavens, back to the planet of her birth.

No. He's dying.

Claire didn't know how she knew this, but she didn't question it. She did as he had told her all those years ago. She closed her eyes, and thought of Max's beautiful soul, about all the feelings he made her feel.

She opened her eyes and found herself in a large bedroom. It reminded her of her parents' old bedroom, in the old house on Hollow Street. This one, however, was much more lavish. It was dimly lit, and several people surrounded a tall bed. A machine beeped slowly but steadily, marking a heartbeat. Claire rose above the crowd, and saw a man lying in their midst, with covers up to his waist.

Max?

The man who lay there looked more like an Egyptian mummy than a living, breathing person.

She reached out with all her senses, and found the love of her afterlife before her. "Oh, Max..."

She hovered above him, and ensured no one around the bed could detect her with any of their meager five or even six senses. She would not disturb them in any way in this emotional time. Her ethereal body would not give them a chill even if they happened to touch her; she could now control such things. Strands of her long, red hair floated at the edges of her vision in a breeze only she could sense, and her white gown billowed around her. Those whom she had met in her journeys told her it glowed with all the purity of lilies in the springtime. The red stain had been left on Hollow Street all those years ago. She had been born anew, just like those flowers.

The people around the room were of all ages. One little boy was the spitting image of a certain little ten-year-old who Claire had often helped with his homework. Surely a great grandson.

She lowered herself so that she could caress Max's face. She closed her eyes, and when she opened them, she was sure he could see her. Feel her. Touch her.

Max opened his eyes.

Several people in the room gasped.

"Dad!" one of the old men said. Claire guessed it was Timmy. Or rather Timothy, as he would probably prefer to be called now. Perhaps simply "Tim?"

"Claire," Max whispered.

She smiled from ear to ear.

"I'm here, Max."

"What did he say?" asked a lady on the other side of the bed.

"I don't know," said Timothy. "Dad? Are you trying to tell us something?"

Max's head fell to the side, and he looked at his son. One corner of his mouth turned up. His voice was creaky, and barely above a whisper. "I'm..."

"Yes, Dad?"

"I'm... going home now, my son."

Tears welled up in Timothy's old eyes. He nodded, and took his father's hand in both of his.

Max turned his head to the other side, and looked into the eyes of all the faces around him one by one. "I... love you all."

Murmurs and cries filled the room.

He turned back to Timothy. "Take good care... of the family, Tim."

"I will. I promise."

Max smiled. "I'll see... you later, kiddo."

Timothy's lips pressed into a tight smile. "See ya later, Dad."

Max then looked up at Claire, and reached out a shaky hand. "Hiya, sweetheart. I'm... ready."

Claire reached out and took his hand in hers.

Max took one last, long breath. His eyes closed, and his body relaxed.

The monitor stopped beeping, and sang a steady tone for a moment before someone silenced it.

An old woman wept softly, and several others, both men and women, joined her.

Claire rose, pulling Max with her. A second version of him, still an old man dressed in striped nightclothes, separated from his earthly remains.

"Claire..." he called.

"Max," she replied, smiling.

The weeping crowd and the darkened room fell away. As Max and Claire rose through the floors of the Butler mansion, he began to transform. By the time they were above the roof and climbing into the starry sky, Max appeared as a young man again. About sixteen, seventeen years old, best Claire could guess.

They embraced as the Earth fell away. A moment later, the space around them flashed, and when the white nothingness faded away, they stood in the center of Max's old bedroom in the old house on Hollow Street.

He looked around, his jaw slack. By the look in his eyes, he marveled at the familiar items from his youth. One poster on the wall displayed cartoonish turtles—"Heroes in a Half Shell", as a young Max had called them with enthusiasm—poised to strike since 1987. She remembered him once saying he had outgrown the cartoon, but that he just hadn't been able to bring himself to take the poster down. On another, Jedi and Sith brandished weapons from a more civilized age. On a third, small letters spelled out "FOO FIGHTERS" over a giant Flash Gordon-style ray gun.

On his old study desk, the Intel Pentium II computer he had labored over while writing school essays displayed rotating images of favorite photos he had either "uploaded" or found on a then-new medium called "The Internet." Claire now understood all of these things, how they worked, and even what they might mean for humanity. She was hopeful for a bright future, even though other souls she had encountered on the Other Side did not share her optimism.

In the corner stood the same bed on which she had snuggled with Max on so many nights, trying her best not to freeze him into a solid block of ice. There would be no need for such a piece of furniture, nor for any of the material items in this place, but the nostalgia filled her with a happiness she had not known since the days these things existed as Max saw them now.

"How?" he asked, his voice a whisper. "How did you do this?"

"Don't talk, you silly boy." Claire wrapped her arms around him, stared into his big brown eyes, and kissed him with all the tenderness, wonder, and excitement a first kiss should possess.

Max did as he was told, and returned the delicate sentiment. She lifted him into the air, and they spun in a slow dance. He said nothing, only stared into her with more love behind his eyes than she had ever imagined possible. She sensed his emotion, his longing, his power. She also sensed his lust, and without question, allowed his energy to envelop her completely. Claire returned the overwhelming passion he now showered upon her with all the built-up desire of two long centuries.

Time seemed to stand still around them. It became irrelevant. Hours or even ages could have passed as they shared their love and became as one being. Nothing was said. Nothing needed to be. Claire couldn't read his mind—not yet anyway—but she could read his energy. And it told her all she needed to know. Max and Claire could finally share the secrets of the afterlife, of the Universe, and everything that ever was or ever might come to be.

After a time passed that neither of them could comprehend, they became two distinct beings once again, but their energy would be forever entangled.

She held his face in her hands. "Welcome home," she whispered.

Max caressed her cheek with his hand, with his thoughts, with his entire being. "Claire, as long as I'm with you, wherever that may be, I'm home."

Timeline

1883	Claire Marie Harvey is born to Mr. and Mrs. Chauncey Harvey III
1899	"Discovery"; Claire is murdered by Stephen Branton
1902	"Awakening"; Claire tries to locate her family
1905	"The House"; Claire discovers she's been dead for six years
1975	Sophie is born to Jonathan and Marion Butler
1978	Max is born to Jonathan and Marion Butler
1988	"The Tutor"; Claire frightens Max with the story of her own death
1996	"Departure"; Demon-Claire finally attacks Max, Max leaves for MIT
2016	"Return"; Claire sees Max and Sophie again, Jonathan crosses-over
2058	"A New Family"; Claire meets Brian and Daria Newsom
2059	"The Neighbor"; Claire devastates the lonely thin man

2061   "The Ghost Hunters" trilogy; Max saves
            Claire's soul from Oblivion

2099   "Unending"; Max and Claire finally join
            one another in eternity